W9-BLU-024

By the same author

365 DAYS

WARD 402

WARD 402

Ronald J. Glasser

GEORGE BRAZILLER

NEW YORK

For information address the publisher:
George Braziller, Inc.
One Park Avenue
New York, N.Y., 10016

Standard Book Number: 0–8076–0691–x
Library of Congress Catalog Card Number: 73–79048

FIRST PRINTING
Printed in the United States of America
DESIGNED BY VINCENT TORRE

FOR ALL THE ARROWSMITHS

Foreword

This is as difficult a time for medicine as it is one of achievement. Despite all the successes a kind of leery feeling parallels the public applause, a suspicion that in making things better some things have been made worse, that in learning more too much has been forgotten.

I finished medical school much the same as any other medical student—eager, confident, sure that a year of internship would be all I needed to put the whole thing together. I was wrong. My internship was not the end I expected it to be, but a wrenching beginning.

It had never occurred to me when I was in school that as a physician there would be anything I'd have to face which was not covered in my classes, anything my professors had not yet worked out, or at least would not have warned us about. Becoming an intern was like passing through a curtain into a world that had never been mentioned, a world I was quite unprepared for.

Ready for hearts and lungs and kidneys, I was confronted with a whole person. In the midst of all the familiar precision, of laboratory values and X rays, suddenly there were human concerns: grief and heartache, personal problems, economics, distrust, fears, and even anger. So seemingly well turned out, with all of science to draw on, I found myself stumbling; all of us were, with only our own strengths and weaknesses to get us through.

The story I have tried to tell in the following pages is true. Everything actually happened, though the events did not all occur in the same sequence, or in the same hospital, or to the same people; some I witnessed myself, others I heard of. Conversations are as I remember them; those that took place years ago I've had, of course, to reconstruct, remembering only the tone; some, especially those of the nurses, I've heard so often that by now they all seem to have come from the same person. Names, dates, places have been changed; the characters, in a sense, are fictitious, since each encompasses a number of people I have worked with. The deaths, though, are real; the suffering, the abuses, the misunderstandings—these, too, are real enough. They still go on.

R.J.G.

WARD 402

I

1

Of the year I spent as an intern at University I can say that all of it was hard but 402 was by far the worst. It was the largest pediatric ward in the hospital. Almost unmanageable in length, it took two nurses' stations to run, and even then, because of the number of children and the seriousness of their diseases, medications were often given late, specimens went uncollected, and parents of new admissions sometimes had to wait for hours before any of the house staff had a chance to talk to them.

There were two interns assigned to 402 at any one time; during my rotation it was Lang and myself. After a few days we realized the only way we could keep up with everything was to rotate the admissions, he taking one and I the next. With only two of us we had to be on call every other night, which meant being up thirty-six hours at a stretch, sleeping seven or eight, and then beginning another thirty-six hours. The nights we were on we had to take all the admissions ourselves, so that no matter what system we used we were always behind in the morning, always trying to catch up.

In a way I was lucky; I came on 402 late in my internship. To have gone there fresh and scrubbed right out of medical school would have been almost impossible. Of the two doctors who preceded Lang and me and had come on the ward directly after graduating, one asked to have his rotation changed and the other, frazzled and exhausted, came down with mononucleosis and had to leave the program.

By the time it was my turn I was well into the eighth month of my internship. I had already finished my rotations through the newborn and premature intensive care units, the emergency room, and the kidney and cardiac services. With another three months of electives in radiology, hematology, and neurology behind me I felt I was ready for anything. I thought I had seen it all, that there was not a childhood disease or complication I had not already been involved with or read about. I walked onto 402 that first day feeling quite assured there was nothing left to surprise me.

I was soon to learn there was a great deal left to surprise me.

A little before five on the afternoon this account begins, McMillan, the pediatric resident, had admitted a three year old directly from the emergency room. During the year, especially in the late winter months, we saw hundreds of children dehydrated from diarrhea. McMillan must have thought this one was shocky or he wouldn't have sent him up so quickly.

It was Lang's turn for an admission. He got a quick history from the mother—a week of poor appetite, fever, vomiting, and finally three days of diarrhea—and then took the patient into the treatment room.

When I had finished what I was doing I went to let Lang know I was going to dinner. The place was a mess. There were discarded needles, IV tubing and alcohol sponges all over the floor. The kid was shrieking, and the nurse and one of the aides were holding him down while Lang was angrily reaching in the drawer for another IV needle. He must already have stuck the child a dozen times, and, to judge from the parts of a surgical cut-down tray scattered on the floor with the rest of the junk, he'd missed a cut-down, too. He looked ready to blow his stack.

"Hold it," I said. "It's my night on anyway. I'll finish up."

For a moment I thought he was going to ignore me. Interns don't like giving up; there's a kind of mystique that makes it hard for you to admit you've failed, especially when it's as simple a matter as starting an IV. Then, too, as interns on the same ward we did have a kind of rivalry going. But Lang had been on the night before, and up for almost all of it with a new diabetic; he was worn out. I guess even his pride couldn't keep him from wanting to get some sleep, so he finally gave up and let me take over.

Everyone has bad days during his internship, times not so much when your mind doesn't work as when your hands just don't seem to do what they're told. Mostly it's because of tiredness, and on 402 we were always tired. Still, even so you can work things out if you're practiced enough.

I'd had my own trouble with spinal taps, real trouble, so I'd gone down to the morgue and practiced on cadavers until I worked it through. The facility I gained with spinal taps spilled over to starting IVs. I was known to be good at it, even with newborns, and I suppose this was one of the reasons Lang was willing to stop.

"I'm not leaving you much," he said, taking off his gloves.

In truth there wasn't much left. He'd destroyed every big vein in the child's arms and legs, even going so far as to ruin the smaller superficial veins on the back of the hands and feet, not to mention the cut-down site on one leg which he hadn't even bothered to suture shut. But at least he'd left the patient exhausted, so that when I bent over the table to examine him he hardly moved, much less resisted.

After ten minutes of searching for a vessel I was beginning to think I'd have to do a cut-down on the other leg when I found a small vein behind the child's ear. Lang had overlooked it, or thought it was too small to use. I took a tiny scalp needle, and threaded the tip of it down under the skin and finally into the vein, made sure it was working, than taped it down. I had the nurse set up the IV bottle and left the room to write up the orders.

To have been scrupulously correct about ward responsibilities I should have called the resident, McMillan, let him know the difficulty Lang was having and that I'd taken over the patient. But I'd cared for enough dehydrations to know exactly what to do, and once I got the IV going there was no reason to call. If after nine months of pediatric internship you don't know how to write fluid orders you should quit and do something else. So despite the fact that McMillan should have OK'd my taking over, I decided not to bother him, to do what had to be done, and tell him later.

2

There are some residents you would have had to call, if only to keep them from climbing all over you when they found out what you'd done. McMillan wasn't like that; he let you alone to do your work. If he felt you didn't know something, or if you told him you were a bit shaky about a procedure or treatment, he'd be right there to show you how to do it. The next time he would watch you do it yourself, and after that you were on your own. If you screwed up, though, if you told him something that wasn't true, or tried something you were unable to do or knew you'd have trouble handling, he'd nail you to the wall and keep you there the rest of the time you were on the ward with him.

If you didn't step beyond your ability he was fine—more than fine, he was exceptional. As tough as he could be and as strict as he was, he was liked by everyone—at least we all enjoyed working with him. He was smart, really smart, and he read more than any other resident on the house staff, even those with more seniority. There wasn't a pediatric or medical journal he didn't at least scan. If he wasn't on the wards, or in the clinics, he would be in the library or having an article Xeroxed in the pediatric office. When he didn't know something he said so, but when he gave advice you knew you could believe him; he didn't have to show off or guess to maintain his position, the way some of the other residents did. Then, too, he had a way of being cheerful without being irritating, and candid without being cruel, though his concern for excellence did make him seem distant at times.

McMillan had been my resident six months before, when I was on kidney service. I certainly didn't know much, and working with transplants and all their complications made my inexperience even more obvious and me more nervous, so that I really leaned on him. But it was what happened right at the beginning of my rotation with him that made me realize how tenacious he could be, and concerned.

I had come on the kidney service a day or two after McMillan, so in a sense we both inherited Kerry at the same time. Inherited is the right word, because the child had been passed on from one set of interns and residents to the next. His hospital chart ran to over nine volumes. Most of us considered him to be a kind of medical and surgical triumph, but we also agreed he was almost impossible to care for. With no kidneys and more than half of his small bowel removed Kerry was always ill; even when things were relatively stable there were at least ten or twelve things to watch for or to check on. We were always waking him up to draw a blood sample, or check his blood pressure, or do an EKG, yet things still got out of hand and his hospital course went from one crisis to another.

With all the testing and blood-drawing it was understandable that the child might be difficult to handle, but that didn't make it any easier to work with him. All kids tend to get freaky when they've been hospitalized a long time, but Kerry was almost unapproachable. Off and on he'd been hospitalized for twenty-two of his forty-seven months, and he showed it. He was not only miserable physically, he was sullen and resentful, and no wonder. By the time McMillan and I got to him he had already gone through a complete kidney transplant, its rejection, months of post-operative care, chronic dialysis, infections, and two cardiac arrests. Now he was back in the hospital again to get ready for a second transplant.

You just couldn't fool him any more, and that made taking care of him all the harder. Everything had been used on him and used again until they no longer worked, all the ploys and the cute little phrases, all the explanations you rely on to get through difficult and unpleasant times, the lies and pleasant deceits you get used to hiding behind and having people accept. Kerry would have none of them. He was not yet four years old but he was as knowledgeable about hospital methods and procedures as any adult. He knew that mornings meant he would be stuck, that trips off the ward to the labs and X ray meant pain, and that a doctor, no matter how concerned or kind, always did something to him. He would glare at you as if demanding to know why, and while he no longer screamed you knew that even though he held out his arm to let you get a blood sample you only got it because you were bigger than he was. And if you failed, if you hooked a machine up wrong, missed a vein, or made any kind of mistake, he'd be on you, yelling for another doctor who "knows how to do it." It was unnerving in a child of his size. He knew how to make it tough for us; and refusing to take his medicine, vomiting up his food, soiling his bed, or pulling out his IVs didn't help to endear him to anyone.

McMillan, though, went out of his way to spend time with Kerry and to talk to his parents who seemed as worn down by his behavior as we were. But as the resident on the service he didn't have to struggle with the kid every day. I did, and no matter what else happened or even how I felt, Kerry was always there waiting for me. I got to the point where I dreaded having to make morning work-rounds. Then just when I was getting as freaky taking care of him as he was to take care of, a kidney became available. It was with a feeling of relief that I watched him being wheeled to the operating room for another transplant.

He came back to the ward alert and active but with his eyes tightly closed. We tried to get him to open them but he refused, and when we checked with the recovery room they said he hadn't opened his eyes up there either, not even when the anesthesia was first wearing off. I thought he was just being his usual obnoxious self, but despite our coaxing and threats he kept his eyes tightly shut, his lips sealed in grim, almost desperate, determination. I suppose he knew that if he opened his eyes everything would be back the way it was before.

As the days passed with no change I became worried about the possibility of Kerry's condition becoming chronic. I told McMillan we had to get those eyes open even if it meant taping back the lids. He didn't like the idea. He was afraid that if we used force Kerry might simply refuse to see; then we wouldn't only have an obstinate kid on our hands, we'd have a case of hysterical blindness.

I was embarrassed that I hadn't thought of this possibility. The truth was that I just wanted to get his eyes open and the whole thing over and done with. As an intern, with so much to do, you tend to look for immediate solutions, but I could see that it would have been a bad mistake to force Kerry's eyes open. McMillan consoled me by saying he might have been tempted to do the same thing if he hadn't happened to come across an article on hysterical blindness. I accepted his support gladly, although I knew he wasn't the sort who just stumbled across important facts. He'd probably researched the whole damn thing the first time he saw Kerry with his eyes closed. In any case, it was plain the patient wasn't going to cooperate; each day the depths of his self-imposed darkness increased. What I and everyone else on the ward had at first thought to be another of his obstinate pranks was settling into a behavior pattern.

It was really spooky to see him sitting propped up in bed blindly, even cheerfully feeling across the cover for a toy he'd dropped or a half-eaten piece of candy. He seemed happy. His thin face, so long drawn into a grim suspicious scowl, had relaxed and taken on a playful elfishness that made him for the first time look like the little boy he was.

McMillan talked to a few of the psychiatric residents, but they hadn't much to offer. Finally we sent in a formal psychiatric consultation request. The staff psychiatrist came by and agreed that something had to be done and mumbled about reassurance and reality testing, but when McMillan pushed for a program he had to admit that he really had nothing to offer.

We tried everything, even going so far as sedating Kerry, putting him to sleep and standing by his bedside when he woke up, in the hope of catching him with his eyes open. It was no good; he awoke with his eyes as tightly closed as when he went to sleep. It began to look rather hopeless and I found myself drifting to other patients and concerns that I could do something about. Not McMillan though. I'd catch him at all times of the day standing by Kerry's bed, watching the child move through his own self-imposed darkness. How he came to do what he did is still beyond me. It must be the stuff miracles are made of.

One night—it was a little before midnight—he woke Kerry up, talked to him and played with him for a while to make sure he was fully awake, then put a small kitten on the bed. I wasn't there at the time, but the next day Barbara, the RN working nights, told me what happened. When the kitten began to move, she said, Kerry suddenly stopped everything and literally held his breath. Then tentatively he reached out to where the kitten was stumbling across the bed covers, and finally touched it. The effect was electric; Kerry gasped and almost jumped out of bed.

"It's a kitten," McMillan explained, and Kerry, trembling, began to stroke the soft warm fur. It was too much for him; he simply had to look. Forgetting everything, the hospital, the pain, the fears, he opened his eyes.

I suppose it shows something of the distance I've come if I admit that when Barbara told me what had happened, my first thought was it was pretty slick of McMillan.

3

When I finally did call McMillan to let him know I had taken over Lang's patient he got on me more than I thought he should have. He grilled me about what I had done and how I had done it, and then made me get him Lang's number at home. I suppose he was right to be angry. After all, he had sent an almost shocky child up from the ER and Lang's fiddling had added two hours to the kid's dehydration. I didn't feel he was angry so much about my taking over without letting him know, as he was about Lang's going so long without asking for help, but he was sore enough for me to keep my feelings to myself and just give him the number. Poor Lang, I thought as I hung up, he's in for it.

It was almost eleven that night before I had everything on the ward enough under control to be able to return to the doctors' station. I checked the temperature sheets and began writing a progress report in each chart. Even if there was nothing more to report than "doing well" or "no change," if McMillan was still angry in the morning, seeing everything up to date would help to soothe him. Scrupulous attention to detail, he insisted, that was the crucial factor in being a good doctor.

When I finished I called the paging operator to tell her I was going to the on-call room, checked the new admission to make sure the IV was still running well, and left the ward to try to get some rest.

I don't think I ever made it through a full night on call for 402 without being waked up at least twice; none of us did. For the most part it was just some little thing gone wrong, like an IV being pulled out, a child spiking a temperature, somebody throwing up, or a morning pre-op order that hadn't been signed. But it could just as well be a true emergency, and then it wasn't merely a case of getting up, going to the ward for a few minutes, and getting back to bed. It meant working the rest of the night.

There wasn't much point in getting undressed. You just lay down on top of the bed, half-asleep and half-awake, waiting for the phone to ring. If you did manage to fall asleep it was always a fitful kind of thing, easily shattered, and in the morning you woke up almost as tired as you were when you lay down. Inevitably you became a bit hardened and discriminating about what you would get up for and what you wouldn't, no matter how serious the nurse who called you seemed to think the situation was. With sleep a priority you learned that even in medicine there were things that mattered and things that could wait. You had to be careful though. If someone's worried enough to call, McMillan said, it's important enough to get up and check. Most of the interns and even some of the residents thought he was crazy to insist on this but in the main he was right. When you checked you usually found things a little worse than you'd thought.

The phone rang about three in the morning. I had fallen asleep without turning off the light and I woke with the overhead bulb burning in my eyes.

It was McMillan. "Sorry," he said. "We've got a new admission."

"OK, OK," I mumbled, sitting up and rubbing my eyes. "What is it?"

"A leukemic."

"How old?"

"Eleven."

"Bleeding?" Holding the phone to my ear with one hand, with the other I groped under the bed for my shoes.

"No, she's not bleeding," McMillan said.

"Fever?"

"No."

"What admission for her?"

I could feel McMillan hesitate. "First," he said.

"What the!—" I couldn't believe it. "Did you say first?"

"Yes, first," he repeated, almost apologetically.

"Wait a minute, man," I said. "It's three in the morning. I've been working every other night for almost five weeks.

I mean I'm tired. She's not infected, she's not bleeding, this is her first admission. Why the hell couldn't it wait six more hours?"

"Prader wants her admitted tonight."

"But why?"

"He just wants it that way."

"That's because he's in bed."

"I'll have coffee for you," McMillan said to mollify me.

"I don't want any coffee, damn it!" I said and slammed down the receiver.

I walked down the corridor feeling abused. A brand new leukemic. There was no sense bringing her in at three in the morning, even if Prader was head of hematology. She wasn't bleeding and she wasn't infected; there was nothing we would be doing at this hour that couldn't wait until morning. Five or six hours more wouldn't mean a damn thing. I was sore, my stomach felt queasy, and every step I took down that empty corridor made me angrier.

I pushed open the first of the ward's double doors. The ceiling lights were off and the night lights gave barely enough illumination to see across the tiled floor. McMillan was waiting just inside the second door and I almost ran into him. Right off I began complaining when something in his face stopped me.

"Something wrong?" I asked.

"No—not really," he said, pushing his hand through his mop of black hair. "It's just—she's really bad. How many leukemics have you taken care of?"

"Three. Why?"

"This is my eleventh. They're all dead," he said softly. "Every one of them."

It was hardly a surprise to me. There was something else on McMillan's mind, behind what he was saying.

The lights near the nurses' station had been turned on, and now I saw a man and woman standing by the desk, looking in our direction.

"Her parents," McMillan said. "She's in the treatment room. Name's Mary—Mary Berquam. You want to do the physical, or take the history first?"

"If she's sick enough to be admitted at three in the morning, she's sick enough to be examined first." I let my voice carry so the parents would hear, and know how annoyed I was.

The treatment room was always bright, but after the muted night lighting on the ward the banks of overhead lamps were dazzling. On the table, barely filling half its length, lay a little girl in her nightgown, her eyes closed, her skin the same lifeless color as the sheet she was lying on.

Barbara was standing by the cabinets, setting up the examining tray.

"Is this the new admission?" I asked.

"That's her," she said. "That's Mary."

I looked more closely at the child, at her wasted, exhausted body, and noted the obvious effort it was for her even to breathe.

"Are you sure?" I said. "This is supposed to be a first admission."

"That's her. Like I said."

"But she looks like she's been sick for months."

"She has been."

"But—"

Barbara shook her head. "Ask her parents," she said sharply. "The tray's ready. I'll be in the drug room if you need me."

"Hold it—"

But she was already out the door. I pushed the tray over to the table.

"Mary," I whispered. The child hadn't moved since I came into the room. "Mary."

She turned her head slightly and opened her eyes. She looked so ill, her eyes were so dull and lifeless, I thought surely McMillan must have been mistaken about her never having been admitted before.

"I'm your doctor," I said. "I'm going to examine you. It's not going to hurt. Honest. I just want to listen to your heart and feel your tummy."

As weak as she was she still tried to help, bending her arms when she thought she had to, even trying to sit up when I wanted to listen to her chest.

"No, no," I said. "It's OK, honey. Just rest there. I can listen without your moving."

She was so obviously uncomfortable I examined her without taking off her gown to avoid any unnecessary movement. Her lungs were clear, her pulses full; her heart sounds, while loud because of her thin chest wall, were normal. I pressed as lightly as I could to feel her stomach, but even that made her grimace. Her liver and spleen literally filled her whole abdomen; I was astonished how big they were. It was impossible to believe that any doctor would let her get that sick without treating her. Surely, I thought, she must have been seen and admitted somewhere before.

"OK, Mary," I said. "Just a blood pressure and we're done."

But she had already sunk back into her state of exhausted lethargy. Wrapping the cuff around her arm I began inflating the balloon. As the column of mercury slowly rose in the manometer she groaned. I took the reading and began to unwrap the cuff. It had become stuck and I had to give it a slight tug to pull it off. Without warning, without even opening her eyes, she screamed. I was startled, unnerved.

"I'm sorry," I said quickly. "I didn't—" and stopped, with the sudden realization that she had screamed in her sleep.

Carefully I removed the rest of the cuff. Her arm was so thin I could feel the bone right under the skin. Though I pressed lightly her face flooded with pain.

"My God!" I said to myself as I left the room to find McMillan.

No one was in the hallway. The nurses' station was empty. I went to the admissions area but nobody was there either. Then I saw McMillan's tall figure coming toward me down the corridor from the little-used conference room. I started to tell him he must have been mistaken about this being Mary's first admission when he stopped me with a question.

"How is she?"

"Sick," I said.

He nodded grimly.

"Not only is she exhausted, wasted, anemic, but she

has bone pain. I mean real bone pain. She's been sick a long time."

"I know," he muttered. "I know."

"She must have been treated some place. She had to be. It's been months at least. The leukemia's all over her body. Her liver and spleen are gigantic. It's in her bones. You sure you got the history right?"

He was about to say something when the hematology technician came off the elevator.

"She's in the treatment room," I said. "I'll fill out the lab slips later. Just get a smear, white count, and hematocrit now."

I looked at McMillan and thought he was nodding in agreement, though he seemed so preoccupied I wondered if he had even heard me.

"Bone marrow?" the technician asked.

"Yes, might as well. We'll—"

"No," McMillan said.

I began to protest.

"No," McMillan said again, more determinedly.

"Look," I said, "I don't care when we do it, but that bone marrow is going to have to be done. She's sick and she's not going to get any better—if she can get better—until we treat her, and before we can treat her we'll need a bone marrow. We're up now, the technician is willing to do it, the patient's already in the treatment room—"

I saw I wasn't getting through to him. "OK," I said to the technician, who was standing by, "Just the smear, white count, and hematocrit."

As she turned to leave I caught sight of Mary's parents standing in the doorway of the conference room. I had the feeling the Berquams had been standing there in the shadow watching us all the time we were talking. Now the father approached us.

"Doctor!" he said angrily, blocking the technician's path.

"Stay here," McMillan told me, and went to speak to Berquam.

I couldn't hear what they were saying but they were plainly arguing. From the conference room came the sound of Mary's mother sobbing. Berquam kept shaking his head obstinately, while McMillan as obstinately kept talking.

"What about it?" the technician said. "I've got other work to do."

"Go on," I said. "Just get a sample."

"You sure?"

"Go. Just do it," I said impatiently. I had no time for goofy parents. Come the morning, we'd need that smear and white count or Prader would be all over my ass and McMillan's, too, but mostly mine.

Berquam stared angrily at the technician but let her go by. He listened a while longer to what McMillan was saying and, still shaking his head, he said no! loud enough for me to hear him.

I heard McMillan say something about at least giving her a chance, but Berquam merely shrugged it off. For a moment I thought Berquam looked more amused than angry, although amused is hardly the right word. Contemptuous is more like it.

4

I had dealt with parents of leukemics before, not as many as McMillan, certainly, but enough to feel that they all behaved about the same. They tried to be helpful, were aware of our efforts and duly appreciative of what we were doing. Even through the last few admissions they acted as if everything was going along alright, and death was not a certainty—only to fall apart at the end and cry so bitterly, when we came to tell them their child was dead, that we could not help wondering if they had ever realized their children were mortally ill. Yet they continued to act deferential towards us, and even contrite.

Berquam was different. He wasn't listening to McMillan, much less agreeing with him; he wasn't asking, he was telling. McMillan was cool, waiting for his chance to say something, then trying again, but it was plain he wasn't getting anywhere. For a moment I thought of trying to help, but then I decided to keep out of the argument, it would probably only make things worse. Anyway, no matter what happened, Mary still had to be taken care of, a chart had to be made up and the lab work signed for; a complete physical still had to be completed, orders written, and a problem list made out.

Somebody had to do all this and I was the one. A resident like McMillan had time to argue, and Prader and the other professors sitting at home or in their labs had time to decide when to admit or when not to admit, but that was because there were others to do the work that had to be done. Like that smear and white count. In the morning I would be the one who was responsible for anything medical that hadn't been done.

I found Barbara in the back, near the narcotics cabinet, drawing up the four A.M. medications. I asked her if she could get Mary into a room.

"Why not?" she said, without looking up.

"You sore about something?" I asked.

"No, it's just that every now and then a parent—"

"Or parents."

"Yeah, parents." Barbara sounded disgusted. "Anyway, I'll get her into a bed."

As I walked back to the doctors' station I noticed that Berquam and McMillan were still at it. Exhausted, with that sick rubbery feeling of having been up too long coming over me, I sank into a chair. It was too late to think of going back to sleep, so I pulled a new chart out of the rack, put my feet on the desk and began writing Mary's work-up. If it had been earlier I would merely have written a quick admissions note and the orders, and finished the work-up the next morning before blood rounds, but now I thought I might just as well get the whole thing over and done with while I was at it.

Leaving the first page open for McMillan's history, I began the second page with Mary's physical examination: the huge liver and spleen, the bone pain, the generalized wasting away, the large lymph nodes, the way she had tried to help, her pale mucous membranes and anemic skin. At the bottom of the page I scribbled my impressions—"acute lymphocytic leukemia"—then turned to the orange order-sheet. For the most part the orders were routine: vital signs every two hours for the first day; diet as tolerated; weight every day; chest film, urinalysis, and urine culture. After the order for the white count, smear, and differential, I wrote "done," so the nurses wouldn't make the technician come back up again. Under medications I left the space blank, and signed both sheets.

The medications would be a problem. They always were. We had protocols for new leukemics. Once the diagnosis was made and the base-line blood studies drawn, the patient was put under one of four different treatment regimes which were selected at random. The protocols were as much a matter of research as they were of treatment, although in truth the only thing that leukemic research had bought, with its new techniques and its ever increasing armamentarium of stronger and stronger drugs, was time.

Nobody really knew which combination of drugs, or in what dosages and what order, gave the best results. Under a national program, Prader and other hematology professors across the country had set up the protocols to find out. Some of the combinations were tough on the kids, for a time making them sicker than they were with their leukemia. But, as Prader said, there was no choice. No one yet knew what treatment regime was best, and if a few weeks of severe iatrogenic illness for the patient advanced our knowledge, proved us right, or meant a longer remission, that was the price that had to be paid. Prader was pretty hard-nosed about it. He was hard-nosed about everything, but staying with the protocols was his first priority. "Stick with the study," he demanded. "No matter how you may feel about it, there's no other way to get the information."

If I'd heard him say it once I must have heard him say it a dozen times. That was another reason I was so annoyed when McMillan told me that Prader had instructed Mary's parents to bring the child in at such an unlikely hour. We wouldn't be able to put her on the protocol study until morning anyway; the protocol cards and treatment numbers were unavailable at night. To keep things from getting fouled up Prader kept them locked in his lab. For that matter, treatment of a newly-diagnosed leukemic had never been an emergency that couldn't wait a few hours.

So I left the medication space blank and was going into the problem list on the next page when Barbara walked in.

"The lab tech sent this up," she said, handing me a slide. "She's rechecking the white cell count. She said the differential will take a while yet."

"Thanks," I said. "If anyone wants me I'll be in the back looking at this."

It didn't take a hematologist to read that slide. It was

all there, brilliantly stained for anyone to see. The whole microscopic field was filled edge to edge with wild misshapen cells. I moved the slide to look at another field. It was the same; I flipped the objective to a higher magnification so I could focus on the cells themselves.

At a 400 magnification a single white cell just about fills a whole microscopic field. I expected to see something textbookish, like the photomicrographs in the hematology journals. Not these. They were the worst I had ever seen. All the subcellular order was gone. The nucleus, stained a crazy, almost shocking blue, was twisted around, rolling in and over on itself. What should have been a homogeneously highly-stained cytoplasm was green and ugly, filled with holes and great clumps of blackish-purple material.

I looked at another cell. It was the same, perhaps even more grotesque. There was something else that bothered me, something beyond the cellular disorder, and when I switched to still another cell I felt even more strongly there was something important here that I should recognize. It was obviously leukemia, but still—

I had made it a habit to look at all the slides I ordered. I was the only intern who did it regularly. Studying the slides was considered technicians' work. Indeed, there were those on the house staff who admitted they felt it was a waste of their talents and time to read lab tests. But it seemed to me that with so much of medicine based on laboratory results they were too important to be left to technicians. It took time, but it gave me a sense of what I was up against. Diseases happen on a cellular and subcellular level and I felt better armed when I could see what I was up against. It also made me a kind of expert on blood smears; if any of the other interns got screwy lab results, instead of going to their residents they would use me as an informal consultant.

This one, though, puzzled me. There was something different about it, something I hadn't seen in other smears, something beyond the cellular disorganization. I was still struggling with the question when McMillan came up behind me.

"What's wrong?" he asked.

"Take a look." I said. "It's from the new admission."

"Later."

"Well, anyway, with treatment we can give her at least, I guess, one remission."

McMillan shook his head.

"What do you mean, no?" I said.

"They don't want us to treat her."

"Then why the hell did they bring her here at three in the morning?"

"To die," McMillan said.

"Hell, they all die. Just like you said. There's nothing new in that."

"Yes, I know," he said weariedly. "The point is, they *want* her to die. They want her to die *now*."

The shocking thing, I suppose, is that I wasn't shocked. We all had our share of difficult parents. With so many children admitted, we were bound to get a few parents who were difficult, but they were never really a problem. A hospital is an imposing place—intimidating is perhaps a better word. Eventually its crisp definitive routines assert authority and even the most hostile parent ends up doing what we want or at least staying out of the way. I couldn't see why McMillan was so worried.

"Want me to talk to them?" I asked.

He shook his head.

"Sure?"

"No, it's—"

"Well in that case, let's get done. The diagnosis is probably lymphocytic leukemia. At least that's what the smear looks like. No matter what protocol we use, we can probably give her at least—You listening?"

He nodded his head vaguely, his mind obviously on other things.

"You don't think we can give her one remission?"

"Oh, I suppose we can."

"Suppose! Jesus! You're not letting her parents get to you, are you?"

"It's not a matter of letting them."

"Why? What can they do?"

"They can keep us from treating her."

"How?"

"Knowledge," McMillan said. "Right now her father knows as much about leukemia as you do. Everything. Everything there is to know."

"He's not a doctor is he? I mean, Prader would have told us that."

"No, just the chief tech, head of the hematology lab at Masonic Hospital."

"Oh."

"Yeah, oh," McMillan said glumly.

"What did you say to him?" I asked.

We had had no formal lectures on dealing with parents.

Each of us was on his own, and as far as I could see McMillan was one of the best. I'd seen him obtain autopsy permissions when the professors had failed, and I'd heard he had never had a procedure denied or for that matter even questioned. If I wanted to be as successful with parents I had to learn how, and the only way was to watch how others did it and understand their mistakes. If McMillan had screwed up I wanted to know why, even if I had to push him, because it was plain he didn't want to talk now. But I had learned during my internship that either you found the answers to your concerns as they came up, or the next day they'd be buried and forgotten under a whole new set of concerns.

"Any coffee around?" McMillan said.

I followed him down the corridor to the kitchen. There was a half-filled kettle on the stove. He turned on the burner and I found some instant coffee in one of the cupboards.

"So what did you say?" I asked again.

"The usual—there are drugs to hold her disease in check and more medications being developed every day; there will be weeks, maybe months, when she'll feel and look normal." He spooned some coffee into the cups. "You know, the usual line about the medications we have now not being able to cure her but still buying time, so that hopefully in the interval a cure might be found or at least more potent drugs. Meanwhile, we would keep her comfortable. The usual thing."

"And he didn't buy it."

"Oh," McMillan shrugged, "he's for keeping her comfortable alright."

"But?—"

"Not for keeping her alive."

"Some father! Jesus!"

The water began to boil, and McMillan busied himself filling the cups.

"She's going to die in any case," I said. "I mean, why let it get to you?"

At the time, I thought I meant it. I had sat through enough conferences on kids with malignant tumors, massive congenital defects, and degenerative neurological diseases—conferences called to see what could be done about additional correctable defects like pyloric stenosis or ureteral reflux—to know that no matter what was decided the doomed were going to die.

"After all," I said, "I mean it's their kid."

McMillan handed me the steaming cup, but his hand shook and some of the coffee spilled on my pants.

"Oh, for Chrissake," I swore, "what's the matter with you?"

"We'll talk about it in the morning," McMillan said. And when I started to object, he added coldly, "I said in the morning."

When I returned to the ward I was surprised to learn the Berquams were still around, in the conference room.

Barbara was in the nurses' station, charting. "They're waiting for you," she said.

"Oh shit," I said. "Not at this hour."

"You know Dr. Prader's procedure. Parents are to stay on the ward until the intern takes a history."

"That's during the day," I said. "In case you haven't noticed it's five o'clock in the morning."

5

Before I left the ward to go back to the on-call room, I checked the IV on the child McMillan had admitted earlier and then out of habit or compulsiveness looked in quickly on Mary. I didn't bother waking her, just watched her breathing, and checked the vital-signs chart pasted on the wall above her bed. Her heart rate, respirations, and temperature ran in three straight lines across the chart—no dips, no peaks. She didn't move and when I looked closer, it seemed as if she was hardly breathing. I think now that I should have tried to wake her—but it was late and I told myself I really wanted to let her rest a while.

It was almost six by the time I got back to the interns room and into the shower. Hopefully the shower would keep me going until after morning rounds and from then on coffee and knowing I'd be able to sleep that night would get me through the rest of the day. After I had bathed, I lay down.

I must have fallen asleep because the next thing I knew the phone was ringing.

Mary was in trouble.

"What are her vital signs doing," I said. I was getting dressed even while the nurse was checking. I didn't run back to the ward. I had done that earlier in the year—the new intern racing down the hallway to save a life—but all I'd accomplished was getting to the ward out of breath and nauseated. So I walked quickly—but I walked. With seizures you have time.

All the lights were on in the ward and McMillan without his lab coat, his shirt sleeves rolled up, was coming out of Mary's room. "I stopped them," he said before I could ask. The orderly was rolling the emergency cart past him into the room.

"What lab tests have you got on her?" he asked.

"Just a smear and urinalysis."

"Better get a blood culture. Did you order any electrolytes?"

I shook my head.

"Better draw some now—Barbara's setting up for a spinal tap."

"Meningitis?"

"No—I don't think so—she doesn't have a fever—probably's leukemic infiltrates in her brain. It could be meningitis, though. Better start an IV too, just in case."

The RN float, who'd come up to the ward to help, stuck her head out of Mary's room. "She's seizing again."

McMillan looked at me. There was a moment of hesitation, then we both hurried into the room. The huge overhead lights were on. The curtain that usually separated the bed from the rest of the room was pulled back. Mary lay naked on her back in the middle of the bed, her body rigid and trembling.

Even as we watched, she seemed to contract for a moment, and then with a visible shudder, her eyes widening, she stretched full length, her head and feet pressing downward into the bed so that her back lifted off the frame. Her body arched higher and higher until it seemed as if her spine must break. Foam welled from her mouth. Then she shrieked and collapsed back onto the bed. McMillan took a vial of Amytal off the cart, cracked it open and drew it into a syringe. Meanwhile, I'd already found a vein and using my hand as a tourniquet held her arm steady as he jabbed the needle into her arm up into her vein, then pushed the plunger carefully a quarter way down the barrel. Even while the medicine was flooding her body I felt her arm begin to twitch. I tightened my grip. We were both leaning over her, our heads almost touching as McMillan injected a few more cc's.

"She's going again," I cautioned.

"That's almost sixty milligrams," he said.

I was having trouble keeping her arm down while he injected more of the medication. It was no use. She was going.

"Paraldehyde," McMillan called to the nurse as he pulled the needle out of Mary's arm.

We gave her the paraldehyde rectally; all of it, over ten cc's. She was half way into her seizure by the time we got the tube into her rectum, but it worked. With the room reeking with the pungent odor of paraldehyde, she suddenly relaxed and slumped back against the bed.

McMillan put the syringe back on the tray.

"Better do the tap now while she's quiet."

"You sure?" I asked. She didn't look very good to me.

"Do you know how much medication she's taken? Half of it would be enough to stop a horse from seizing. There's something going on in her head."

We just dumped everything—the used syringes, IV tubing, cotton balls, empty vials—onto the floor, and broke open the spinal tap tray. The nurse straightened the bed as best she could and then with McMillan she turned Mary on her side with her back towards me. I sterilized her back with alcohol and did the tap. It went smoothly. As wasted as she was, there was no trouble finding the right intravertebral space. The needle slipped easily between her vertebrae into her spinal canal.

The spinal fluid began flowing smoothly out of the end of the needle. I would have taken off more fluid but it looked like she was beginning another seizure, so I pulled out the needle.

When they let go, her body twitched again, but it stopped short of a seizure.

McMillan was rolling down his sleeves. He shook his head as he looked compassionately at the stricken child.

"What's her smear like?" he said.

"OK," I said. "There are some bad-looking cells, though."

The main lab was down two floors. The night technician was not around so I set up the spinal sample myself. There are a number of tests that are routinely done on all spinal fluid samples, but the important one was the bacterial stain. I divided the sample of spinal fluid and put one part away for the sugar, protein, and culture determinations; the rest I smeared on a slide to look at under the scope. It takes three minutes for the dye to take; when it had set long enough I took the slide off the staining rack and, using the distilled water over the sink, carefully washed off the excess color. Then clipping the slide into the frame I looked through the lens and cranked the slide into focus. I could make out the grains of dye fixed to some dirt that had stayed on the slide, but no bacteria. I checked another field, and then another—and then quickly scanned the whole slide. Her spinal fluid was negative for microorganisms. Even those one or two white cells that might or might not have been considered as part of the normal fluid were absent.

McMillan wasn't often wrong; when he told you to look for something it was usually there. I went over to the reagent shelf, took down the bottle marked bromosulfophthalein, and picked up the second part of the spinal sample. I was taking a chance screwing up the culture, but with no bacteria on the smear and no white cells it was hard to believe that the fluid would grow out any organisms. If there were cells that for some reason I'd missed there would have to be protein too—abnormal amounts. So I measured out four cc's of the bromosulfophthalein and, opening the sample of spinal fluid, poured it in. If there was any protein the bromosulfophthalein would precipitate it out of solution. For a moment the two fluids mixed and then dissolved one into the other, but nothing came of it. I held the sample up to the light; there were no particles settling out—not even a hint of precipitate. That amount of reagent would have precipated out any protein in the fluid, even trace amounts. The spinal fluid was normal—there was nothing there: no cells; no protein; nothing.

While I was shaking the tube and holding it up to the light, the technician walked in. She carried her own samples to the work bench.

"That's spinal tap fluid—or what's left of it," I said.

"It's opened," she said. "We wouldn't be able to culture it."

"I know. Just do a sugar on it."

"Who's it on?" she asked.

"The new leukemic."

"Oh! I'm sorry, I haven't done the white count yet. I'll do it now."

"Don't hurry. We won't need it till morning rounds."

"Was that man who stopped me her father?"

"Yes. He was just upset. He'll be alright in a couple of days."

As I climbed the two flights of stairs back to the ward, through the windows I could see the dawn lightening the sky. I found McMillan sitting on the desk in the nurses' station, the phone balanced on his shoulder. Down the corridor the light in Mary's room was still on.

"Nothing," I said.

"But there must be cells."

Holding up his hand, he stopped me from talking. "OK, OK, OK," he said. Shaking his head he hung up the phone. "You sure about the smear?"

"Yeah."

"How much fluid?"

"About two or three cc's."

"Did you use the new stain?"

"I used the one that was there."

"I don't know," he said. "She's still seizing."

"What about her electrolytes?"

"Normal—that's what I was on the phone about. I've given her just about the whole damn pharmacy. Hell, this doesn't even happen with brain tumors." He frowned. "Where's the stain on her spinal fluid?"

"Down in the lab. It's negative."

"Could you get it?"

"Look," I said, "I know how to make stains."

"I'd like to see it myself," McMillan said.

"That's not going to change anything. Looking at it up here won't make it positive."

"I know," he said impatiently. "I just want to see it."

I felt pretty sore about McMillan's questioning my competence. He could really get to you at times. For a moment, on my way down to get the smear, I thought of going back to tell him if he was so damned worried he'd better do everything himself, maybe call a neurologist—or Prader, for that matter.

Of course I didn't. Not because I was afraid to set him off, but because I knew he wanted to make sure; I was that way myself. Besides, Prader would probably ask him if he'd looked at the stain; at the very minimum he would demand a differential diagnosis of what could be wrong.

There was a small library next to the lab. It wasn't much of a library—no journals, just a few reading desks and a couple of shelves of books. I picked two of the newer textbooks of pediatrics, and opening them to the chapters on neurology, quickly ran down their lists of convulsive disorders. In both texts the lists ran to over a page and a half, but all the items fitted somewhere under the six usual pathological classes: poisons, tumors, congenital malformations, vascular disorders, infections, or metabolic defects —we'd screened for all of them. In one way or another the blood and urine tests we'd ordered, and the spinal tap I'd done, covered every class. If there was something making her seize, it wasn't in those lists.

I got the stain from the lab and took it back upstairs to McMillan.

He was writing down more lab results. "Did she look dehydrated to you?" he asked as I handed him the stain.

"A little, but more wasted than dry."

"Well, she can't concentrate her urine. The lab just called with her urinalysis report. The specific gravity on her sample is low. If she was dehydrated she'd be concentrating her urine—trying to conserve water."

Bothered, McMillan took the stain over to the microscope.

"Is this Mary's peripheral smear?" he asked. "This slide already on the scope?"

"It's the one I looked at earlier," I said. "I guess I left it here."

He sat down and looked at it. "Did you look closely?" he said, adjusting the fine focus.

"Yeah, remember? I'm the one who told you it was lymphocytic leukemia."

He switched to another field. "How closely did you look?"

"I looked at it closely enough to make a diagnosis. Want me to tell you what it looks like cell by cell? The cytoplasm is a dark grainy—"

"It's not the individual cells," McMillan said. "Here, take a look."

"I did, damn it," I said. I was too tired to be pushed.

"Then look again," he said, and when I made no move, "Look, will you!"

It was the same smear I had looked at before.

"Well?"

"Cells," I shrugged. "Lymphocytic leukemic cells."

"How many?"

"A lot."

"They're packed," McMillan said. "Not just a lot. There aren't even any spaces between them. It's just one solid sheet of leukemic cells."

I looked back into the scope. He was right. Absolutely right.

"Jesus!" I felt my confidence in my own ability, so hard won, suddenly dissolving right there in front of me. I had missed the main thing. I had fixed on the individual cells and ignored the overall picture. After nine months of internship, to misread a simple blood smear!

"Her white count must be over three hundred thousand, maybe even half a million," McMillan said gravely. "She's suffocating inside out. All those white cells are sticking together, blocking up her smaller arteries, stopping the blood flow to all her organs. That's why she's seizing. The problem's not in her brain but in the capillaries that feed it. That's why her kidneys can't concentrate her urine. They're not getting enough oxygen. Her bone pain—Everything's affected."

"I'm sorry," I said. "I really am."

McMillan wasn't interested in my apologies. "It's called a blastic crisis," he continued. "For some reason the body just unloads billions of leukemic cells into the circulation. It's rare, but it happens."

"I should have picked it up, though," I said apologetically. "It's right there on the slide, for God's sake. A medical student could—"

"It's over," McMillan said. "It could have happened to anyone."

I shook my head in disagreement.

"Now you know," he continued, "you won't make that mistake again. Right? OK," he said dismissing it, "so what should we do now?"

I was still so disturbed by what I had done, or rather hadn't done, I could hardly think let alone talk.

"Come on," McMillan said impatiently.

"Get rid of the cells, I guess, and open up the vessels."

"What would you use?"

"Prednisone."

"And what else?" He waited, and when no answer was forthcoming, he added, "Allopurinol. Do we have any here on the ward?"

I was still so awash in self-criticism and embarrassment, it took a while for what he'd said to seep in. Then it hit me.

"Wait a minute," I said. "You going to do it?"

"That's right."

"But that's the same as treating her leukemia. I thought

you said her parents didn't want her treated."

"I'm treating her seizures," McMillan said calmly.

"But treating her seizures in this case is the same as treating her leukemia. I mean it's all the same. You're going to open up her vessels by destroying all the abnormal leukemic cells. That sounds like the same thing to me."

"If she came in bleeding we'd give her blood, wouldn't we?"

"Sure. We feed kids with leukemia and give them water to drink. But that's not treating them."

"This is an emergency," McMillan said, with a touch of impatience in his voice. "If we don't open her vessels she may not have a brain left when we get her into remission."

"OK, OK, I'm convinced. But what about Prader? Prednisone's on every protocol. If you use it tonight differently than the schedules say—well, he's not going to like it."

"He's up in the lab and we're down here."

"You're the boss," I said. "But he's still not going to be happy."

I wasn't too happy about it myself. Even when things were going well Prader was tough; when they weren't, he could be impossible. There were times when his moods affected his responses, so that what was worth a twenty minute harangue one day might be handled with a simple discussion the next. Then, too, there were times when he seemed merely capricious, as when he insisted on having a white cell count on one patient repeated, while the week before he'd let it go on a patient with exactly the same illness. Or he could get angry with you for not having all the red blood cell indices ready when you were treating a patient with iron deficiency anemia when the day before he'd lectured that in most cases of this type of anemia the smear itself was enough for the diagnosis.

All of which made things a bit more nervous and difficult, because you never knew for sure which way Prader was going to jump. There was no doubt in my mind, though, about how Prader would react to McMillan's treatment of the new patient. He wouldn't like it at all. McMillan might at least have called him, and I think at the time I assumed he had. It was only later I realized he hadn't.

The prednisone we gave Mary destroyed the billions of leukemic cells clogging her vessels, but that didn't mean we cured her disease, any more than stopping her seizures meant saving her life. If the treatment of leukemia is difficult, it is not because the individual leukemic cells are resistant to medications, but because the overall disease itself—the sheer mass of abnormal cells—obeys first order chemical kinetics. Concern and suffering aside, it is eventually the physics of cellular destruction that beats you. It is impossible to destroy every leukemic cell; no matter what drug you use, in what combination or over what period of time, there are always a few that escape.

No one really knows why. In his lectures Prader attributed treatment failures to the fact that the medications never reached some of the more remote cells, those hidden away in the recesses of organs. Hematologists at other centers disagreed with him, holding that the first order kinetics was due not to sequestration of a few cells but to the development of some kind of cellular resistance to the drugs themselves. The only thing that everybody did agree on was that a few leukemic cells hidden away in some poorly perfused part of an organ, hiding in a capillary or venule, managed to escape destruction and, continuing to divide, eventually broke out again, repopulating the entire body with a whole new series of leukemic cells.

McMillan knew this—he probably knew it better than any other resident in the hospital—but that didn't stop him. He even drew up the medications himself.

It took us over five minutes to inject all the prednisone, and then using the same vein, merely changing syringes, another five minutes to give Mary the allopurinol. Before we had quite finished she began twitching again.

While we watched, helpless, having already done everything we could, the whole left side of her face started trembling. She was still unconscious, but her left eye and the corner of her mouth were twitching in a kind of grotesque wink. Then as suddenly as it had begun it faded away.

"Well," I said, relieved, "that's one for our side."

"It's a beginning anyway," McMillan said, allowing himself the first smile I'd seen all night. "Come on, let's get some more coffee."

In the cafeteria we milked the urn for the last two cups and took them over to the side of the room still set up for the night staff. Yawning, McMillan stirred some sugar in his cup but hardly took more than a sip.

I was still fretting about that smear. McMillan said I'd never miss one again, but that was small comfort. I was too conditioned by the attitude fostered in medical school and nurtured there, that with all the machines and new techniques, with lab values read out to milligrams percent and X rays that can show almost anything, there is no reason to make mistakes. I was beginning to see that medicine was not that simple. Even if you knew what had to be done there were still the trade-offs, the morbidity from the treatments themselves, and these gray areas of when and how much. And then there was the business of putting it all together and holding on to it. I'd heard about blastic crisis, I'd read about it, I knew about it, but at 4:30 in the morning it simply had not registered.

What do you do about things like that? Work harder? Read more? Ask more? Missing the smear might have been humbling if it had been acceptable. Well, I thought, at least my night on duty was almost over. True, there was still a whole day ahead, but with daylight at hand you can begin to think about the end of the thirty-six-hour stretch, and that makes it almost over.

McMillan was stirring his coffee aimlessly, lost in thought.

"Why don't you clean up?" I said. "It will take a while to get all the bloods drawn before rounds."

"Very well," he said. "I'll be back up about quarter to eight."

He got up to go and I left soon after, when I had finished my coffee. You get a kind of second wind in the morning. No matter what happened during the night, no matter how tired or pushed you felt, or maybe even abused, it still buoyed you up to know that while others were sleeping you'd been working, doing what had to be done.

II

6

The day nurses and aides were already on the ward. Crowded into the nurses' station they were taking reports from the night shift. Lang, in a clean set of whites was leaning against the wall, listening. When he saw me he left the nurses and followed me into the doctors' area.

"What's with the new admission?" he asked.

"Which one?" I said, fishing through the file cards for the name plates I needed to stamp out the morning lab slips.

"The new leukemic." He pointed toward the nurses. "They seem to be taking sides."

"What are you talking about?"

"Didn't McMillan treat a leukemic who was almost dead?"

"She wasn't almost dead," I said defensively.

"Well, did you treat her?"

"Yeah, I guess so— In a way."

"What protocol did you use?"

"We didn't," I said.

"You didn't!"

"It was an emergency, for Chrissake. Besides, it won't be hard to put her into the study. Every protocol has prednisone as one of the drugs."

"Sure," Lang said skeptically, "but part of the study is how the drugs are given, and this hasn't been Prader's month for being kind to the house staff."

"Well, anyway, it's done."

"Maybe, but I'm glad I wasn't on last night."

"Let's get going," I said, "or we'll never get all the bloods finished."

Even with everything going right on 402 it was still a struggle to get the bloods drawn on time. We drew daily lab tests on almost every patient on the ward. Despite the medical school emphasis on physical examination, and the lip service given physical diagnosis, that was the kind of medicine we practiced. When a patient coughed, we might listen to his chest but the demand was always for the X-ray results. On rounds, and in conferences, it was the smears and white counts that were discussed, the creatinine clearances, the BUNs, the alkaline phosphatases, phosphates, sodium, potassium, magnesium, specific gravities, sedimentation rates, complement levels, differentials, eosinophil counts, Comb's tests, hapteglobins, PHs, acid-base balances, blood gases. We didn't just order the tests to have them in the charts; they were what we focused on.

We lived with their daily ups and downs, gearing our treatments, fears, and concerns to their fluctuations.

"I don't know how he feels; he can't be better with a sed rate of over a hundred. . . . Push the steroids till the complement levels are normal. . . . Keep him on penicillin till the white count comes down. . . ."

We watched the numbers. We used them to monitor our medications, confirm our impressions, or make us change our minds. An 8.1 instead of a 7.9 became more important than vomiting, diarrhea, or even pain. In what could have been a confusing world of symptoms and complaints the numbers pointed the way. They made our work precise and sometimes even unarguable. They kept us from ever really being surprised or thinking we could be. It was comforting to be able to say fifteen hundred instead of a thousand. And so each morning Lang and I, like interns everywhere, gathered the blood samples on which everything seemed to turn.

If we could have split up to draw the bloods it would have been quicker, but there were so many small children on the ward we had to work together and help each other. Some of our patients—the cardiacs and birth defects—were so tiny we had no choice but to do jugular or femoral sticks to get the blood. Even starting fifteen or twenty minutes early we never would have finished on time without the help of Mrs. Gowan, the chief nurse. She usually got to us halfway through our blood drawings, when her own nurse's report was over.

Mrs. Gowan had been an RN before quitting to get married. She had raised her two kids past kindergarten and then, finding herself bored with housework, had come back. She was about twenty-eight, as smart as she was good-looking, and returning to work because she wanted to, not because she had to, gave her an independence and freedom that was refreshing, if at times hard to take. It was a struggle to run 402 properly, and if she felt pushed or that her nurses or aides were being abused she'd let you know. With all the problems of patient-load and inadequate staffing, she still managed with a minimum of fuss to keep it all together, pitching in herself whenever she felt her help was needed. She was so competent it was hard to remember she was only a year or two older than Lang or me, but that was all she was and it kept everything loose and open.

When Mrs. Gowan joined us that morning we had just finished struggling with a three year old who had shrieked at the top of his lungs and fought us the whole time we were drawing his blood. Lang literally had to lay himself across the child to hold him steady, with the kid screaming the whole time almost directly into his ear, while I drew the blood. When we walked out my ears were tingling, and Lang could hardly hear.

Mrs. Gowan was in the corridor, straightening up the top of the blood cart.

"Could have used you in there," Lang said, shaking his head to clear his ear.

"You'll get better at it," she said.

"It's my ears I'm worried about."

"They'll get better at it too."

Lang grinned. Mrs. Gowan was too pretty and feminine for him to accept her readily as the accomplished nurse she was. He considered himself a ladies' man, and he was, but 402 had put a damper on his playing around. At the beginning of our six-weeks rotation he had tried to continue with everything he'd been doing on the other, less busy, wards—making day-time dates for coffee, visiting nurses on other wards, spending his nights off with his girl friends. It didn't take more than the first week for him to realize that the demands of 402 were extreme; the time required to get everything done did not allow for anything but medicine. He took to making phone calls from the ward. "Just to keep things going," he said with a wink, "till this rotation's over."

I had my own concerns—a nurse I'd met just before I came on 402; we'd sort of agreed to put everything in abeyance for the six weeks I was on the ward. I didn't think she liked the idea and I know I didn't, though I did feel a bit righteous telling her how necessary it was if I was going to do 402 right. In truth, from what I'd heard about the ward I could see no other way, and as it turned out there really wasn't. We did manage a few quick dinners together, but that was all. When things got extra rough I consoled myself with the thought that only a few more weeks and we'd be together again.

At the beginning of our rotation Lang seemed a bit bemused by Mrs. Gowan's efficiency, especially when she became angry enough to get on him to get things done. As the weeks passed his bemusement became a kind of flirtatiousness. Mrs. Gowan could handle it, but she was probably counting the number of days Lang had left on 402 as much as he was.

"Have you got to Johnny yet?" she asked now.

"Who?" I said.

"The child with dehydration who was admitted last night. On report Barbara said his IV was a little behind."

"How much behind?" Lang asked.

"Hundred and fifty cc's."

"That's not much," I offered. "It was a small needle." Lang didn't look convinced. "It's OK," I assured him. "He got enough."

We pushed the blood cart farther down the corridor, past the linen closet to the next set of rooms. Lang picked up a five cc syringe and said he'd get the dehydration himself.

I didn't argue about it. If he wanted his patient back he could have him. Technically the child was mine, but we still had three weeks to work together and it wasn't worth making a fuss. 402 was hard enough as it was; to start letting egos get in our way would have made things intolerable.

I picked up another syringe and went with Mrs. Gowan into the room across from Johnny's. We came out before Lang was through with his patient. Mrs. Gowan held the sample tube while I emptied the syringe into it. I took the needle off the syringe and threw it into the discard box.

"I suppose you heard," I said, although I knew, of course that she must have learned what happened from the night staff's report.

When she made no sign of having heard my remark—she could be very tight-mouthed when she wanted to be —I asked her if she'd seen the new admission, and suggested we both go in to see the patient.

We paused just inside the doorway. The window blind

was down, but the morning sunlight angled in between the slats. Mary looked so wispy as she lay there on the bed not moving, her eyes closed, her drawn face delicately etched on the pillow. Tired as I was and hard-nosed as I thought I'd become, I simply had to stop and stare at this lovely little girl.

"We'll need a white count," I said, breaking the spell.

Back in the corridor again Mrs. Gowan said: "I'm told the parents didn't want her treated." She handed me the white-count tube. "They were quite definite about it, at least to the nursing staff."

"True," I said.

"But you did, anyway. And without the protocol."

"Correct."

"Did either you or Dr. McMillan contact the parents to let them know your plans, or what you were doing?"

"No." I put the tube in the sample rack.

"Why not?"

"Because it was an emergency."

By the time Lang and I had finished drawing the bloods McMillan was on the ward, going over the nurses' report with Mrs. Gowan and reading the problem sheet. When we had labeled the last sample, she took the blood tray off the cart and, letting the three of us alone to begin work rounds, took the samples into the nurses' station to separate them for the various labs.

Morning rounds with McMillan were really work. Some of the other residents, indeed most of them, used the rounds just to keep themselves up to date, so all we had to do was tell them what was going on with the patients. Or they used them as a way of showing off by getting into long tortuous monologues about most anything from urine cultures to the Heavy Chain diseases. McMillan kept his rounds patient-oriented. What were we doing to find the diagnosis? What had gone wrong the day before? What could go wrong? What were our plans for the day? What complications did we expect? These were his concerns, and we had to be thinking the whole time. When he had to, he'd dwell on a point, but discussions that would have taken longer than a few minutes he left for later, or for the scheduled conferences. We were there to make sure the day would go right, that was what the mornings were for, and he insisted they be used that way. If at times our rounds dragged a bit it was because he also insisted upon seeing every sick patient and reexamining them himself, even if it was the tenth morning in a row. For the most part, though, the rounds were quick and helpful—to Lang and me as well as to the patients.

This morning the ward was pretty much under control and we moved through the patients quickly. McMillan cautioned us about the complications from a few of the drugs we had ordered, talking about hypertonic dehydration when we got to Johnny, and recommended additional lab tests on some of our more difficult diagnostic cases. As we went along he kept adding to his own records, mostly concerns about what he thought were deficiencies in nursing care, which Mrs. Gowan was usually able to explain away when she joined us. She asked if he was still planning the bone marrow on Mary we'd ordered the night before and he said he was.

"Have you got permission?" she said.

"No."

"Don't you think you should?"

"It's not a surgical procedure."

"I know, but don't you think in this case?—"

McMillan shrugged off the suggestion. "It's a routine procedure."

"It could be helpful," Mrs. Gowan said, "during report—"

"Look," McMillan interrupted, "there's no need for a consent."

She seemed surprised at his abruptness. It wasn't like him to ignore procedures.

"Maybe not in the formal medical-legal sense," she said. "But these are concerned and difficult parents, and no matter what you may think, my nurses are going to have to deal with them."

"We'll all have to."

"Then don't you think it would help to start off right?"

"OK," McMillan said. "We'll get you one."

"It's not for me," Mrs. Gowan said.

We were down at the far end of the corridor discussing that morning's last patient when Mary's father came on the ward. Lang and Mrs. Gowan were facing the other way and McMillan simply didn't see him. I just happened to look up as he was opening the door to his daughter's room. A moment later he was back in the doorway, searching up and down the corridor until he caught sight of us. He was livid.

"Doctor!" he barked.

Startled, McMillan looked in his direction and Mrs. Gowan and Lang turned to see Berquam charging toward us. An aide who at that moment was stepping out of a room, carrying a specimen, bumped into him and he pushed her out of his way so roughly the tube fell from her hand. Leaving the spilled specimen where it had fallen she started after him angrily, only to be stopped by McMillan.

"It's alright," he said, keeping between them. "It's alright."

"Son-of-a-bitch," she swore. "I'll—"

"What the hell's the meaning of that IV?" Berquam demanded.

"It's alright," McMillan assured the aide again, ignoring Berquam's question. "It'll be taken care of. Just go on with what you were doing."

Reluctantly, still glaring past McMillan at Berquam, she moved to go.

"What the hell's the meaning of that IV?" he demanded again, his voice strident with anger.

McMillan waited until the aide was some distance away before he turned around to face Berquam. "This is not the place to discuss your daughter's condition," he said. "Nor to knock people around." And when Berquam was about to protest, "Not here," he warned. "If you want to talk, I'll talk with you in the conference room."

Berquam had no choice but to follow McMillan down the corridor. He slammed the door shut behind them.

"Jesus!" Lang said.

"Was that Mr. Berquam?" Mrs. Gowan asked.

"Who?" said Lang.

"The father of the new leukemic," I said.

"The one you treated?"

"Yeah. Mr. Berquam in person."

"Christ! He's nuts— Is that the guy you were worried about?" Lang asked Mrs. Gowan.

She flushed. "I believe you are referring to the child's father," she said.

"Come on," I said. "Let's finish."

But that closed door was like a bad thought which kept intruding, and I kept looking in its direction, waiting for the storm to break. Still, ten minutes later, when the door opened and McMillan stepped out, he didn't look too bad to me.

"Well?" I said.

He picked up the vital-signs chart. "We'll wait for Prader," he said calmly. "Now what about the new cardiac?"

We worked on as if nothing had happened. Prader would set everything straight; I was sure of it. There were a lot of things I was sure of then, and Prader was one of the surest.

7

I felt certain Prader would not tolerate Berquam's behavior. But then he probably wouldn't go along with McMillan's not using the protocol, either, or my not having the bone marrow ready. Exact, organized, demanding, he was a difficult man to please, but any thought you might have that he was harassing you personally, or persecuting you, was quickly squelched by the recognition of how hard he worked himself; also the fact that no matter how much he abused you, you came out of it knowing more than before he went after you.

Which didn't mean I liked him. You could respect Prader, but it was hard to like him. There seemed to be an unnecessary edge to everything he did; he never let up. We all speculated on why he behaved the way he did; when there was nothing else to do it was always good for a five or ten minute rap. Some of the older residents, those who had known him longest, thought it all had to do with his research concerns, that in a sense the ward was another lab to him, and at the time I agreed with them. He was a full professor, one of the three or four in the whole department, but unlike the others who had begun their promotion through their research and kept going through their politicking or administrative skills, he had stayed with his research, if anything getting in even deeper as his clinical responsibilities grew.

As a hematologist Prader had originally been interested in white blood cells. For years he had worked in his lab exploring the metabolism of leukocytes, publishing papers on the effects of drugs on cellular processes. Eventually his work took him into the chemistry of antimetabolites and finally into the use of these drugs in leukemic cells. Gradually his lab became a center of leukemic research. Physicians from all over the country began to ask his advice and then, under his federally-supported treatment program, to send him their leukemic patients. In response to the patient referrals, the hospital expanded the number of pediatric hematology beds and made Prader the head of hematology.

His organized lab was a far cry from the chaos of a pediatric ward, but he became a superb clinical hematologist, building one of the largest clinical services as well as research areas in the whole hospital; and one of the most closely run. Right up to their deaths, his patients were the most painstakingly worked-up and followed of any service.

I had already been involved with a few of his patients. It was at the beginning of my internship, during my hematology elective, and I remember his demanding, even as a child was bleeding to death, that the lab values still be obtained and the results documented. I had watched interns draw white counts on children so bloated they could hardly move, and do bone marrows on patients who had in effect been abandoned, because there was nothing more to do for them. I stood beside him by their beds and listened to him lecture on white-cells inhibition and bone-marrow depression while the children whose disease we were discussing were dying in front of us.

It took a while to get used to. I never once saw Prader waver. He simply went on teaching, directing, pointing out, no matter how pathetic the child looked or how ill. His research fellows up in his lab said they could tell when one of his patients died; he became even more demanding than usual, more critical about their work and their results. On the ward, though, it was hard to know. He gave no signs of strain and his moods didn't seem to correlate with his patients' conditions. He'd get on the house staff just as hard when everything was going well on the wards as when they weren't. It was only later I realized that many of his patients died at home with none of us knowing but him.

Part of my hematology elective was to sit in on an initial interview with the family of a newly admitted leukemic. The American Board of Hematologists had originally recommended such an interview, and Prader had made it a part of each new leukemic's work-up. With his usual thoroughness he insisted not only that the interview be given within twenty-four hours of admission and as close to diagnosis as possible, but that every resident, intern, and medical student on the hematology service sit in on at least one. He called a series of staff meetings to decide on exactly what should be covered, so that each interviewer would deal with essentially the same topics and in the same way. As regimented as the whole thing was, it still filled a need, although some attributed Prader's concern with the parents not to any humane reasons but to his wanting them to stay with the study until the end.

Usually the interview was given by the full-time senior hematologist assigned at the time to the clinical service. During my elective it was Prader himself.

The interview I attended was exactly what you would expect from him: logical, ordered, meticulously thorough. After introducing Bradley to the parents as the intern on the ward, the physician who would be responsible for their son's daily care, he explained the positions of the various doctors they'd be meeting. Then, "I don't know what you've heard about your son's illness," he said, getting up from his chair, "what preconceived notions you may have. Whatever they may be I can assure you that his disease is like any other illness, subject to the same scientific laws, consequences and treatments."

Using the blackboard at the front of the room, he described the normal developments of their child's hematological system. He drew the outline of a bone and filled in the center as he talked. "Every red cell or circulating white cell in a person's bloodstream comes from cells developing in the bone marrow. And the marrow produces not only red cells to carry oxygen and white cells to fight infection, but also another type of cell. These cells," he explained, turning to face the parents, "are called platelets and are absolutely necessary to stop you from bleeding. Sometimes—and we don't know why—the normal controls regulating the bone marrow differentiation of these three types of cells are lost. Then the whole bone marrow factory gets turned on to producing only one kind of cell—an abnormal white cell. The bone marrow soon fills up with them and eventually they overflow the bone marrow space and begin flooding the whole blood stream, eventually infiltrating every tissue of the body. For some reason—and again we don't know why—these cells are not only produced in too great supply but are themselves abnormal, unable to do what they should do as white cells—that is, fight infection."

I noticed how closely Prader watched the parents as he spoke. He stopped a number of times, even going back to explain things he must have felt might still not be clear to them. At the same time he seemed to go out of his way to itemize and even to dwell on the complications that could be expected by this take-over of the white cells.

"Anemia will result because red cells are no longer being made, and bleeding will occur because platelets are no longer available to stop it, and even though there are billions of white cells being produced, infections will be a problem. Anemia, infections, and bleeding, these are the complications. We expect them, and have available therapy."

Prader didn't mention the pain from the leukemic cells getting into the nerves and bones but he did talk about the changes exerted on the body by the runaway production of such a mass of abnormal cells—the wasting of normal tissues, as nutrients were diverted from them to white cell production, the difficulty the child would have (with so much of his protein intake being shunted into white-cell production) in making normal amounts of necessary proteins like antibodies and clotting factors.

Sitting in the back of the room, as I listened I could forget he was talking about an afflicted child. He seemed to be talking about a machine breaking down, explaining the disaster by showing how this valve got clogged and that one was overwhelmed.

It worked, though. In the course of minutes, without conjuring up big words or concepts, he'd removed all the mystery and managed, by mechanizing the whole thing, to hold out hope where there was no hope at all, to calm parental fears without in any way diminishing them. Even as he talked I could see the parents gradually relax in the security of knowing what had happened to their child. It was all just a matter of one type of cell pushing the rest out of the way.

"Our therapy," Prader continued, "is aimed at destroying these abnormal cells, eliminating them from the bone marrow, blood stream, and any other organs they may have lodged in. By getting rid of them we give the other three types of normal blood cells enough oxygen, nutrients, and room to begin to grow again, take over the blood stream, and do their job. We have medications now, and more potent ones are being developed all the time. Hopefully, we'll have a major development during your son's illness. That's part of the work we're doing right here in our own labs. Unfortunately, at the present time, while the drugs we have are very powerful, they are not one hundred percent effective. They do work, though, and while they are effective your son will be able to live an absolutely normal life."

Leaving the blackboard Prader went back to his table. I thought the conference was over and was about to get up to leave, but to my surprise he sat down again. Even more surprising to me was the way he sat for a quiet moment looking down at his hands folded on the table. Then, raising his eyes, instead of talking further about bone marrow, cellular differentiation, or caloric shunting, he spoke about families and relatives, about grief and guilt.

"This will be a difficult time for you," he said softly. "Believe me, honesty and frankness will be our most important weapons and crutches; indeed, they will be absolute necessities."

Then, unfolding his hands, he reverted to his former matter-of-fact tone. "There are a few things you should be aware of. First of all, this is not a familial disease. We don't know what causes it—probably a virus or a lack of immunological control—but whatever it is, it is not genetic and it does not run in families, nor does there appear to be a carrier state.

"Nothing you have done or have not done is known to contribute to the development of this disease—not smoking during pregnancy, excess vitamins, diet patterns or anything else. Your friends may, and probably will, make comments that will seem inappropriate and even critical of you as parents. You will simply have to remember that such remarks are made in the hope of being helpful, and accept them as such. I can guarantee that your son is getting the best possible care. Again I must caution you not to blame yourselves; nothing you could have done would have made any difference. An earlier diagnosis would in no way have changed the picture."

Thinking about the interview later I realized Prader had not once mentioned the word leukemia. At the time I was impressed by what seemed to me his unexpected consideration for the parents and his concern with the nonmedical aspects of the disease. But then that same day, after the interview, he chewed Bradley out in front of me for not getting a chest film on the child he'd just discussed.

8

As a rule, we saw Prader only during his formal hematology rounds on Wednesday afternoons and Saturday mornings. Dr. Sharf, an assistant professor in neurology, was our daily attending, while the rest of the hematology group—whoever was available at the time—came to help out on the emergencies, or problems that came up between Wednesdays and Saturdays.

Prader's rounds were really something. The only relief was that he was as tough on his own staff as he was on us. He knew everything that had happened since his last rounds, and he spent a good part of each of his sessions grilling his own research fellows as well as the house staff about why we had done what we did. His knowledge of hematology as a whole, not only his own field of leukemia, was phenomenal. He read literally everything on the subject and had as personal friends all the real experts in the various fields of blood disorders. He served as editor on several hematology journals, deciding on what should be accepted for publication and what rejected, so that he not only had important information in advance of almost everybody else, but knew what had already been tried and hadn't worked. You simply couldn't beat him; most of the time you just listened and tried to defend yourself.

McMillan was the only resident who regularly stood his ground. My first week on 402, midway through Prader's conference, I saw McMillan, who was sitting in the back of the room, raise his hand. The room was packed; it always was on Prader's rounds. The hematology staff alone almost filled it, so with the ward personnel, medical students, and doctors from the other services crowding in to hear and to learn, many including myself had to stand.

McMillan was sitting so far back that Prader at first didn't see his raised hand. Lang had just finished presenting a patient with anemia secondary to kidney failure; the child was on dialysis awaiting a kidney transplant from his sixteen-year-old brother. Prader lectured a few minutes about the uremic causes of anemia and then questioned two of the transplant surgeons present about the prudence of using a sixteen-year-old donor. They saw nothing wrong with it and Prader agreed that the risk seemed justified, since the brother was the only decent immunological match available. He was going on to the next patient when McMillan, apparently tired of holding his hand up for notice, interrupted.

"I have to disagree," he said.

Everyone turned to look, some even getting up from

their seats to see who had the nerve not only to interrupt Prader but to question him.

"There is a risk," McMillan said.

"We know that," Prader said.

"A significant risk."

Prader leaned back in his chair. "And just what is that risk?"

"Dying," McMillan said. "The recently published transplant registry shows there has been one death in a donor—"

"Yes," Prader cut in irritated. "But the risk is the same for any donor, any age—"

"And morbidity," McMillan continued unruffled. "A greater risk from injury. The older brother is an active adolescent. If after giving up one kidney he has an accident—say an injury in sports—that could damage his remaining kidney he'd be a transplant candidate himself. An inactive adult is not at the same risk."

"Do you have any data, Doctor?" Prader asked.

The two transplant surgeons visibly relaxed.

"Yes. There have been six thousand kidney transplants done in the country, three thousand with cadaver kidneys and the same amount with those of related donors."

Prader remained silent as McMillan went on: "We know that the mortality is at least one per three thousand. The morbidity is harder to assess since the complications to the donors, at least the late complications, are not yet entirely in. It does seem, though—"

I noticed that the two surgeons were looking less and less relaxed as Prader allowed McMillan to go on without interruption. "Well, Doctor," he said finally, "what would you recommend?"

"Protecting the donor. Using a cadaver kidney, or even a poorly matched adult donor."

Prader looked at the surgeons. "What do you think of that?" he asked.

"Well, sir," one of them offered, "a matched donor kidney has a much better chance of taking."

"Not true," McMillan countered. "If the donor is an identical twin, maybe, but an unrelated donor or a cadaver kidney, with the use of decent immune suppressive therapy, has the same risk of rejection as a related donor."

The surgeon hesitated, and looked at Prader as if uncertain what to say.

"I'd like to see the data," Prader said. "Please bring it to my office this afternoon."

That ended the discussion. The brother was never used as a donor.

During his own year of internship McMillan had taken, as I had, an elective in hematology and then, like any other intern, had had ward assignments where he was responsible for Prader's patients. Prader had never seemed to bother him; at least the interns in his group said he gave no evidence of being bothered nor, apparently had Prader ever been able to intimidate him.

"It's the way he teaches," McMillan explained to me. "Some guys are nice about it, some are hard-nosed. As long as you learn, it doesn't really matter."

And then, of course, Prader must have known about McMillan. All the professors knew who the brightest interns were and prided themselves on their accomplishments, and McMillan had been by far the brightest in his group.

After the episode about the donor, though, I noticed that Prader would occasionally go out of his way to question him and push him on some really rough material. McMillan always did well. Once when he was a bit fuzzy on the mechanics of the hemolytic anemia in Lupus Eranthematosis, Prader became pickier and pickier until neither McMillan nor anyone else in the room had the answer. McMillan didn't panic. He said he didn't know, and then, before Prader could get to him, asked for the references so that he could look up the answer. Prader, taken by surprise, suddenly found himself on the receiving end and had no choice but to give the references—which he did, then and there, from memory. After that, he seemed to be more lenient with his younger colleague.

Even though his formal rounds were only twice a week, Prader rounded himself on each new leukemic patient the morning after the child's admission. It was a ritual he never missed, and if he happened to be out of town at the time, he came by the first morning he was back. If the parents were around he would introduce himself but he wouldn't go out of his way to look for them. All he did was read the patient's chart and then look in for a moment and leave—after setting up the protocol, that is. But he could have done that by phone.

On the morning after Mary's admission he must have gotten to 402 a little after ten. I was passing the nurses' station to get some X rays when I saw him. He was standing by the rack reading Mary's chart. For all the confidence he generated, and the worry and concern his presence inspired, he was not physically an imposing-looking man. Of average height, his thinness made him seem taller than he was. His hair, mostly in a thick ring around the back of his bald head, was black, as were his eyebrows, without the slightest touch of gray. He must once have been considered good-looking, in a skinny sort of way, but right now as he stood there reading Mary's chart he was just plain business-looking.

When I came back he was still behind the glass, holding the chart as he talked to Mrs. Gowan. She looked mighty sober to me. We're in for it, I thought, as I hurried by the station before he could see me.

Lang was in the treatment room, using the view box to look at some chest X rays. He was about to put up another film when I came in.

"He's here," he said.

I didn't need to be reminded. "Just check the X rays," I said. "I want to use the view box."

"He sure came up somber. Like he's getting himself ready for the onslaught."

"Don't act so disinterested," I said. "You'll be close enough to get some of the spinoff."

Lang shook his head. "I know. That's what's bothering me."

"Come on," I said impatiently, "I've got to look at these. Finish, will you."

"OK, OK, if you're in such a hurry— If I were you," he said as he was leaving the room, "I'd stay in here for a while."

It took only a few minutes to look at my films, a follow-up IVP on a child who'd been admitted a week before, uremic from massively infected kidneys secondary to an obstructed bladder. He'd already been operated on. His kidneys were so bad—there was so little tissue left—that the surgeons, hoping to protect what little remained, had completely diverted him, draining what urine his kidneys could make into a bag on the outside of his body.

The X rays looked terrible—small shrunken kidneys with big dilated tubes leading into the ileostomy bag—but at least the situation wasn't any worse than before the operation. If you pushed a bit, maybe it was a little better.

I put the X rays back into their folder, and went down the corridor away from the nurses' station. I should have taken them to the nurses' area where they could be returned to the X-ray department, but I was anxious to avoid Prader as long as I could, so I carried them with me and went to tell the child's mother what the X ray showed.

I found Mrs. Leroy standing by her boy's bed.

"How do they look?" she said.

"Alright," I said, reassuringly I hoped. "Better anyway."

The child was sitting up, opening one of the presents she had brought him.

"Do you think he'll have to be operated on again?" she said, almost timidly.

"No, I don't think so. The place where the urine comes out—the hole through his skin—may with time contract and have to be revived."

I was sure the surgeons had already explained to her what the operation had entailed, but the word "hole" seemed to frighten her.

"The surgeons explained, didn't they?" I said.

She nodded, but she still looked apprehensive.

"Did you understand?"

"A little," she said in a way that told me she didn't.

I should have known, I thought. There were times when I had trouble keeping up with some of the surgeons. "Here, let me show you," I said. I took out my notebook and drew a diagram to show her what had been done and what I meant about the stoma contracting. I didn't show her the X rays; none of us ever showed parents the studies themselves. It was a kind of informal tradition that you were to interpret what the lab results revealed, not show the tests. The idea was not to make the parents nervous with technical details they were not prepared to understand. That it could also be a device to keep control, to keep the mystery—and patient respect—alive and working, had not occurred to me then.

I had not quite finished explaining when Prader walked in. He didn't waste any time.

"Excuse me for interrupting," he said to Mrs. Leroy. "Could I see you for a moment, Doctor."

He didn't wait for an answer, but turned away and walked out into the corridor.

Mrs. Leroy and I exchanged glances. "I'll be right back," I said.

Prader was waiting for me a few steps down the corridor. "Were you on last night?" he asked. His face was expressionless, but his question sounded more like a demand.

"Yes sir," I said. "I was."

"Did you write the orders on Mary Berquam?"

"Yes sir. And I signed them. They're in the order book."

"You know there's only one history on the chart—Dr. McMillan's."

"Yes sir, I know. It was late and I did the physical while Dr. McMillan did the history. We—"

"So you didn't talk to the parents then."

"No, but—it was three or four in the morning and the child was desperately ill. One of us had to be with her. The parents were obviously distressed and exhausted—"

Prader's face hardened.

"We judged it was better for one of us to take the history," I continued defensively, "than for both of us to put the parents through the same set of questions."

"Did you talk to them this morning?"

"No—Mr. Berquam—"

Prader cut me short. "I know about Mr. Berquam," he said. "I'd like you and Dr. McMillan to be in my office in fifteen minutes."

Round one, I thought as he walked away. He had known everything he asked. It was going to be a tough morning.

When I returned to Mrs. Leroy I found her sitting on her son's bed, helping him put together his toy.

"That was Dr. Prader, wasn't it?" she asked.

"Yes, it was." I hadn't thought she knew his name. "He's not always that gruff. It's just that he's got a lot on his mind." I picked up the folder of X rays I'd left at the foot of the bed. "How did you happen to know that was Dr. Prader? I mean, Gregg's never had anemia or anything like that, has he?"

"No, no," Mrs. Leroy said. "It's just what I've heard

from some of the other parents. He's the world expert on leukemia, they say."

I don't know why I should have been surprised that parents exchanged information, but I guess my face showed I was.

"Oh," she said, smiling, "we parents all talk about the doctors."

I might have asked what she'd heard. Whom she'd talked with. What they said. What their feelings were. That way I might have found out what was happening on the ward. But I didn't ask, because I thought the parents were not my concern, and that anything they might say hardly mattered. We were doing the best we could to take care of their children. That was enough, wasn't it?

The question remained with me as I walked back to the nurses' station. The truth was we had no idea what the parents thought about, and really didn't care. We saw them only as visitors coming and going, or as future nursing aides who would one day be responsible for carrying out our orders. When we talked to them we talked about medicine. Even those of us who became friendly did so tentatively, so as not to become involved. There was too much to do, if parents got in the act we would never be able to finish our work.

McMillan was in the nurses' station talking to Mrs. Gowan when I came in to put the X rays in the return box.

"You know—" I said.

"I know." He looked at his watch. "We still have a few minutes."

"What did Prader want from you?" I asked Mrs. Gowan.

“Data,” McMillan said drily.

“He wanted to see the evening nurse’s notes,” Mrs. Gowan said.

“Nurse’s notes?” I said.

“That’s right.”

“Jesus!”

“Come on,” McMillan said impatiently.

“Did he see Berquam?” I asked as we walked toward the elevator.

“He did.”

“What happened?”

McMillan shrugged. “I don’t know. I wasn’t there.”

“Well, what did he say to you?”

“That he wanted to see us in his office. That’s all.”

“What do you think it’s all about,” I said as we came to a stop by the elevator bank. “I mean, I know what it’s about, but—”

He pressed the button. “The protocol, I suppose.”

“But why the nurse’s notes?”

“Well, you know, he likes being sure.”

“You don’t sound too worried.”

“What can he say? I know what I did, and the reasons.”

“Then you’d better do the talking,” I said.

We had to step aside for the group of nurses coming out of the elevator.

“You mean the answering,” McMillan said.

9

Prader's office was away from the main hospital, in the hematology research area. The elevator opened on a corridor cluttered with equipment. Dented oxygen tanks and liquid nitrogen containers lined the narrow, pitted corridor. This was the oldest part of the hospital. Removed from the patient areas, it had never been remodeled and what changes there were had been made solely for the purpose of utilizing every available inch of space for research. The labs were little rooms off the corridor; the original space had been divided and subdivided until there wasn't enough room for all the equipment, which overflowed into the hallways, making them as much a part of the labs as they were thoroughfares.

As we approached Prader's office at the end of the corridor we had to walk single file to get by the freezers and centrifuges. We could see the research fellows at their benches; several looked up from their work to wave or nod as we passed. We knew most of them; at one time or another they had been on the wards themselves, or at least had accompanied Prader on his visits to the hematology patients. No matter what research his fellows were doing, he required they be there for his rounds.

Prader was talking to one of them when we reached his office, and we waited outside until he had finished. It was the same old office he had held on to since he'd become a professor. The hospital had expanded, new buildings gone up, new departments organized, new office space allocated, but he'd stayed on in the research area. People said he just wanted to be obstinate, but the likelihood was he simply felt more comfortable in the midst of his research.

He was standing by his file cabinet when we walked in, putting away a folder. The office was small and cluttered. Books and journals lined the walls. The desk was covered with papers, and open journals with passages outlined and marked were piled one on top of the other. On the radiator behind the desk were stacks of patient charts reaching above the window sill.

Prader didn't offer either of us a chair. "What do you think of the problem?" he said, closing the cabinet drawer.

I looked at McMillan but he didn't seem about to answer.

"Well," Prader said as he turned to face us, "do you have any plans?"

McMillan still made no move to speak. In the silence I could hear the hum of the equipment out in the hallway.

Prader looked at me. I could feel myself sinking, but I'd be damned if I'd be the one to open my mouth first and get the first blast. Despite myself, my heart was pounding.

"I'm waiting," he said quietly.

"Put her on protocol," McMillan said. "Prednisone is the primary medication for all of them."

At last, I thought, relaxing.

"And you?" Prader said.

"Me?" For a surprised moment I thought of just dropping the whole thing back on McMillan, but I had sense enough to know it wouldn't work. Prader wasn't one for pushing off responsibility.

"Well, sir," I managed to say, "treat her—"

"You have," he said. "That's not the problem."

I thought he might simply be using me to develop some point, but there was nothing didactic in his tone.

"Do you know what the problem is?" he said.

"Yes, sir."

"What is it, then?"

All I could do was stand there, trying to think of something.

"He has nothing to do with what happened last night," McMillan said.

Prader turned to him. "He wrote the orders, didn't he?"

"Signed them," McMillan corrected. "I decided what had to be done."

"In a court of law," said Prader, "he decided."

"Maybe in a court of law. But last night I decided. If he hadn't agreed I would have gone ahead anyway."

Shaken as I was, I still worried that McMillan might be going too far. Prader was the boss and if he found what we had done unacceptable, he could do what he wanted to either of us or both. But except for a slight tightening of the lips, his expression remained unchanged.

"I treated a medical emergency," McMillan said. "I didn't institute therapy to treat her disease, but a complication."

"And the parents?"

"They were distressed. They came in with a dying child who had been suffering at home. They had obviously decided in their own minds that the child was gone or they wouldn't have brought her to the hospital. They had worked out their grief already and they weren't about to listen to anyone. As far as they were concerned the child was dead."

"That's an opinion," Prader said.

"It was my impression."

"And you acted on an impression."

"I treated a medical emergency and formulated an impression about the patient's parents and acted on it."

"You mean parent," Prader said. "Parent," he repeated, and waited a moment to let it sink in. "Mrs. Berquam called me this morning, after your interview with her husband. She was almost hysterical. Afraid we weren't going to save her child. Your impression, Dr. McMillan, was rather incomplete. Histories, if you remember, are taken from both parents."

McMillan flushed, but kept grimly silent as Prader turned to me. "If you are going to be responsible for patients, you had better learn to rely on yourself, not on the people you work with."

I could see McMillan stiffen.

"You are to take your own case histories, no matter how inconvenient it may seem at the time. In case you haven't realized it yet, medicine is not all for the doctor's convenience. Despite what you may have heard, or what may be practiced, it is a twenty-four-hour-a-day business; five in the morning is no different from three in the afternoon. I want the history from the Berquams on my desk this afternoon. Is that clear?"

I nodded my head like a dumb fool.

"They're waiting on 402— As for you, Dr. McMillan, I'd advise that you go back to the ward and try to find out what the hell is going on."

Prader rose from his chair, "That will be all," he said.

Relieved, I was about to make my exit when McMillan said, "And what protocol will we be using?"

"Let's have a diagnosis first," Prader said sharply, making no effort to hide his annoyance.

"The smear is almost unequivocal—"

"Another impression? Or is it an opinion this time?"

A quick flash of temper, and McMillan left without replying.

"Well?" I said, when I had caught up with him. "What the hell happens now?"

"Make the diagnosis," he said.

"You don't seem worried."

"Maybe she doesn't have leukemia," he said sarcastically.

"That's not the point. I don't think that's what's bothering him."

"Whatever it is, it will pass."

"I mean I don't think it's just the protocol," I persisted.

"If it's not now, it will be," McMillan said.

We rode down the elevator in silence. McMillan was playing it pretty cool, but I was sore. To be talked to like that! Like a child! As if I didn't know what medicine was! I had never felt more abused.

Walking back through the main lobby I looked at the clock over the information desk. The business with Prader hadn't taken as long as I'd thought; there was still a lot of morning left.

McMillan seemed at ease as we crossed the crowded lobby, but I was still fuming. Damn Berquams! I thought. As if things weren't hard enough without them. Still, our encounter with Prader could have been much more of a disaster. All things considered, I had got off fairly well. And so had McMillan, despite his inviting trouble.

"Did they get the chest film on that ENT admission?" I asked.

"A portable."

"Did you see it?"

McMillan shook his head. We had to slow down to let a stretcher by.

"There's time," I said. "I'll get that history out of the way, then go down to X ray and see what it looks like. Do you want me to bring it up?"

"Yeah," he said absently. "If it's worth seeing."

The Berquams were in the conference room. Suddenly unsure of myself, I hesitated at the door. As physicians we were used to being respected, even adored. These are attitudes we have come to expect from patients—or, in a pediatric ward, from parents—the starting point of all our interactions. To have to confront parents I knew in advance were hostile, to have that adoration gone at the very beginning, made me feel unarmed, unready. Still, the interview had to be done, and I felt resentful enough to want to get it over with in a hurry.

I introduced myself as the intern on the ward and sat down in the chair facing Mary's parents. Berquam was grim, but he answered my background questions quickly and in detail. As he spoke, his wife leaned forward nervously in her chair, hanging on his every word but saying nothing herself, even letting him answer my questions directed at her about her daughter's birth or her own prenatal care.

"When did you first know she had leukemia?" I asked.

"About three months ago," Berquam answered matter-of-factly, as if I was still asking about the child's immunizational history, or growth and development, or diet.

There seemed to be no point in prolonging the interview or trying to soften the questions. "How did you find out?" I said. "I mean about her having leukemia."

"From the family physician. She was sick for three days. Like everyone else we thought it was the flu. When she started throwing up, we took her to our doctor. He agreed with our diagnosis," Berquam said drily, "gave her six hundred thousand units of procaine penicillin. So we took her home and two days later she began bruising. I called the doctor again, took her back in—We got a smear and white count and made the diagnosis of lymphocytic leukemia."

I asked what happened after the diagnosis was made.

"Nothing," Mrs. Berquam said. "She just got sicker."

Stony-faced, her husband looked down at his hands and then up at me.

"After the diagnosis," he went on as if there had been no interruption, "we decided to let her die in peace. She would stay at home with us as long as possible, and then finally she would die in the hospital, sedated and painless."

Mrs. Berquam was sobbing now, but he made no effort to comfort her.

"Very well," I said, closing my pad. "We can talk again tomorrow."

"Doctor!" Mrs. Berquam cried as I got up to leave.

Her husband put out his hand to stop me. "We want her comfortable," he said. "You understand? Comfortable."

"Doctor!" Mrs. Berquam cried again, as if she was pleading with me to understand more than what her husband was saying.

"Marquette!" he said sharply. Then, more softly, "We've decided, haven't we? We've decided." He turned to me. "We just don't want her to suffer."

"Neither do we," I said. "I assure you, we don't either."

10

The film was in the portable box. I took it into one of the nearby dimly lit rooms, clipped it up on the view box and switched on the lamp. Like most portable films it was not a very good X ray. The heart borders and pulmonary vessels were blurred, and the lung fields themselves had a hazy overall granular appearance. Even the bones were washed out because of the poor quality.

I took my time and went over it leisurely, area by area. After the tension in Prader's office and the conference room, it was soothing to stand there in the cool silence of the viewing room with nothing to worry about except the film.

The X-ray department, indeed radiology itself, had always been comforting to me, even in medical school. There was a precision to X rays that was appealing, almost seductive. It was all there, everything you needed; no frills, no foolishness. I've lost track of the number of times I'd worried about a pneumonia in one of my patient's lungs only to have my concerns settled by a chest film; or the nights I'd wondered about whether an ankle was sprained or broken only to see that thin hair-line fracture on the X ray. Everything unnecessary or superfluous was gone, burnt away by the high-energy beam.

It was pure; the kind of definitiveness that we strove for in everything else. If you knew what to look for and how to look for it; there was little chance of missing the diagnosis. Sometimes after an X-ray conference I'd wonder how the older physicians had been able to practice at all. And then their poor patients—tumors missed, pneumonias untreated, fractures unset or set wrong, osteomyelitis left alone to destroy whole bones, knees injured for life.

I moved closer to get a better look at the film. Even with the poor quality the right lower lobe of the lung looked a bit too hazy. I thought of Prader again. He might complain about procedures and protocols, but he'd complain a lot more if one of us misread an X ray or ignored a low hemoglobin value. And parents too; some of them might fuss about this or that, but they'd be a lot more angry if we missed a fracture and sent their sons home with only an Ace bandage.

I was about to take the film down to use the spotlight on it when the radiology resident walked in.

"Not too good, eh?" he said.

"You mean the technique?" I asked.

"No, that lower lobe."

"It's sort of hard to tell, isn't it?"

"That's not all poor technique. That's an infiltrate. It's just too fluffy. And see the way the haziness moves out laterally," he said, tracing out the area with his finger. "Here, along the rib margins. That's an infiltrate and fairly diffuse. What's his problem?"

"Post operative fever. Had a T and E two days ago."

"Why don't you send him down for a regular film. We can get a lateral view then, too."

"OK. Can I take this up with me? McMillan wants to see it."

"Yeah, it's dictated. Just take the film jacket with it."

"You want it back for the X-ray conference?"

"No hurry. Conference is not till three o'clock."

I took the film up to the ward. Right inside the double doors there were several small groups of parents and visitors standing in the corridor. It struck me as unusual, because it was lunch time when the kids were eating in their rooms and the halls were normally empty of visitors. Further down the corridor I could see more visitors standing in the doorways talking with one another. As I walked by, those nearest me stopped talking; even those farther down the corridor became silent as I approached.

"What's going on here?" I thought. I said hello to several parents I knew and was surprised to see some of the mothers ignore me or turn away. Even those who acknowledged my greeting seemed to do so hesitantly, as if something had come between us. Yes, something was wrong, that was plain, though I had no idea what might have brought about this sudden chilling of the atmosphere; I even thought I must be imagining things.

Chris was in the doctors' station. She was one of the

RNs who worked days. For a while she had been working permanent nights, so that she could take courses at the university. But after surviving a semester of this, plus the social activities of a very attractive young woman, she had given up and gone back on the regular nurse's rotation, with the idea of returning to school full time in the fall. "It was too much," she said. "It seemed like I was going weeks without sleep."

She was a good nurse and liked the kids. Sometimes she would take one of her little ones along with her to the nurses' conferences and keep the child in her lap, playing with him during the whole meeting. She got pretty close to the parents, too, but for the most part, even though she had ideas of her own about how things should be done, she kept to herself. Mrs. Gowan liked her, and obviously trusted her; she gave her as much responsibility as she could, sometimes even putting her in charge.

"Have you seen McMillan?" I asked Chris.

"He's in with Mary," she said, without looking up from what she was doing.

I took the films over to the small view box at the back of the station, and clipped up the films.

"Is her father still around?" I asked.

When there was no answer, I said, "Why the silence, Chris?"

"He's gone," she said. "He was really put out."

"Gone? Gone where?"

"To the hospital administrator."

"What for?"

"What for! To sign his daughter out of the hospital against medical advice."

"Wait a minute," I said. "Is that what's going on out there? I mean with the visitors?"

"You guessed it," Chris said, crushing out her half-finished cigarette in the ash tray.

"How did it happen? I mean did Berquam and McMillan get into it again?"

"Not exactly. Dr. McMillan simply walked into the room and announced to Mr. Berquam that he was going to draw blood for more tests."

"So?"

"He could have done it differently. Instead of just announcing it."

"You don't think Berquam will really sign her out, do you?" I said.

"That's not the point, and you know it. You doctors!"

Chris was plainly in no mood to be reasoned with, so I switched on the view box and went out to get McMillan. He was just leaving Mary's room with a handful of blood-filled sample tubes.

"There'll be no doubt about the diagnosis now," he said. "There's not a reasonably valid test I haven't drawn."

"Did you know Berquam left to sign his daughter out?" I said.

"He was loud enough about it. They must have heard him in the next ward. He was pretty hot."

"Did you talk to him first?"

"No. When I walked in with the syringe and tubes and started to explain, he just went crazy. He didn't give me a chance to talk."

"Maybe you should have, I mean, maybe tried to talk to him first."

"Maybe. But I don't think it would have made any difference. Anything would have turned him on. Besides, what would we have done if he'd said no? Don't worry," McMillan added, holding up the blood filled-serum tubes. "It's when we treat her there'll be trouble. These are just tests."

"Do you think we should let Prader know?" I suggested.

"If you want to. Right now, I've got to get these down to the lab."

I decided against calling. Prader would have wanted to have all kinds of answers. Anyway, McMillan was probably right. It's difficult for a parent to sign his child out of a hospital against medical advice. It happens, but it's rare. The pressure on parents not to sign their children out is fantastic, the greatest being the problem of where to take them after they leave. It's a closed market. Of course I could be wrong. And in that case I wondered if it would not be better in the long run to let Prader know.

I was standing there by Mary's half-closed door, still hung up on what to do, when Mrs. Gowan came up behind me.

"Sorry to interrupt," she said, "but Freddy Handelman's on his way in."

"Oh God!" I said, "that's all we need."

"The emergency room just called. He's a direct admission."

"Have you told McMillan?"

"No, not yet."

"How long before he gets here?"

"I don't know. A few hours, I suppose."

"Have you checked Mary lately?"

"Chris is taking care of her today. Why?"

"Nothing. Thanks. I'll be in with her a while."

Mary was still unconscious. I looked at the vital-signs chart taped to the top of the small dresser near the side of her bed; her blood pressure, respiration, and heart rate ran in three straight lines across the chart—no change. I checked the IV that hung over the bed, watched the drops slowly drip into the tubing, and made sure the needle was still fixed firmly in her thin arm.

Everything was in order, yet I continued to stand by her bedside, unwilling to leave. She looked so delicate as she lay there, so vulnerable, as if the least wind could blow her away. Chris, or one of the aides, had braided her tawny hair into two little beribboned pigtails which lay like wings on the pillow on either side of her head. They seemed too playful for her expression. Even though she slept her lips kept something of their tension, a kind of grim expectancy.

I don't know how many sick children I've looked at, how many I've treated. There are so many, you lose track of them; they come and they go. But every now and then there's one who gets to you right at the beginning, a child with a special magic. You fight it because it makes everything so much harder, but it stays with you. Mary was like that.

I smoothed her cheek gently with the back of my hand and let my fingers touch the edge of her mouth. Unexpectedly, her eyes opened, and without moving her head she looked up at me, barely able to focus.

"Are you going to stick me again?" she said in a faint little voice that despite its weakness was still fearful, and I saw the tears welling up in her eyes.

Maybe I was just overtired, or overwrought, maybe it was just four weeks of 402, or simply how she'd asked and how she looked at me, trying not to cry, or maybe I don't even have to find an excuse, but for a moment there I had to fight back my own tears.

"No, Mary," I said, "I'm not going to do anything to you."

"My tummy feels funny."

"I know—Just close your eyes and rest."

Reluctantly they closed again, and I stayed a while longer watching her breathe.

I found McMillan in another room down the corridor talking with Lang about one of his patients.

"Did you know Mary's awake?" I interrupted.

"Yeah," McMillan said. "She's been coming around all morning."

"She's looking better— Coherent, anyway."

"Well, at least, she's on her way."

"Mrs. Gowan tells me Freddy Handelman is coming in."

"Oh Christ!" Lang said. "When?"

"Soon."

"How many does that make?"

"Three," McMillan said.

"I thought it was four admissions."

"No. There was a cadaver kidney and a living donor. His mother, I think."

"You up?" Lang asked me.

"No," I said. "You are."

"Damn." Lang looked at McMillan. "Anything wrong?"

"I was thinking of Freddy's parents," McMillan said. "They're apt to be a bit hyper—"

Another Berquam, I thought.

"We'll need a renogram for the kid when he gets here." Lang said.

I told them I was going back to the doctors' station and would call X ray and schedule it.

On the way I met the aide whom Berquam had almost knocked down. She was still looking upset and I started to apologize for his behavior.

"I shouldn't have gone off the handle myself," she said.

"You know how it is," I said. "If you're a parent and have a child as sick as his—leukemia—you can get a bit freaky."

"You mean it's like he said? She's going to die?"

"What do you mean, like he said?"

"You know, when he was out there yelling at Dr. McMillan."

"What else did he say?"

She looked embarrassed. "Just things," she said. "I've got to go now," and lowering her eyes she hurried past me.

Just things, I thought as I sat down heavily at the nurses' desk. Things I felt I ought to be more aware of, but wasn't. Like those people in the corridor who seemed to be sharing a secret they didn't want me to know about. And then Chris suddenly acting peculiar, as if she had a chip on her shoulder. And now the aide.

To hell with it. There was too much to do to worry about what people said, or didn't say. I read the typed three-by-five index card pasted at the bottom of the glass partition in front of me. It was the nurses' list of that day's scheduled admissions: Two ENT patients, two urology, one general surgery, two eye patients and one pediatric admission with a possible diagnosis of rheumatoid arthritis. They all had to be worked up, but the pediatric admissions were the ones we really took our time with. All we did for the off-service admissions was a physical to be certain they were ready for surgery, a quick history to make sure the surgeons didn't do anything foolish or inappropriate, and a kind of weary follow-up post-operative.

For 402 it was a routine admission list. Freddy Handelman's coming in simply made it more routine. I made the call to X ray and then crossed off the list on my own notepad what had already been done. Most of the morning's lab tests were still out, so I called for the results. The lab slips came up at the end of each day, but the tests were run around noon, and by calling then I could get a good three hour jump on what had to be done, and the advantage of day-time staffing to help get it done. I usually started with chemistry, getting the day's electrolytes, then microbacteriology for the culture reports, serology, and finally immunochemistry.

11

I had almost worked through my complete list when I saw Mrs. Berquam walk hesitantly on the ward. She was looking around, apparently for someone who might help her. When she saw me behind the glass she gave me a pathetically open smile and quickened her pace in my direction.

"Is Dr. Prader here?" she asked, standing in the doorway of the station.

When I told her no, she looked confused. "He called me at home and asked me to meet him here." She glanced at the clock. "He said twelve-fifteen."

It was almost that now. "He should be here soon," I said. "He's pretty punctual," and added, "Your daughter's better."

"Yes, I know."

"Who told you? I mean, were you here this morning?"

"No, Dr. McMillan called me at home to tell me."

"When was that?"

"A little before lunch. Why?" she said, suddenly frightened. "Is she worse?"

"No, no," I reassured her. "In fact, she's probably even a little better."

"Is my husband here? Dr. Prader wanted to see us both." She smiled diffidently. "I'll be in Mary's room. Is that alright?"

"Sure. I'll tell Dr. Prader you're there."

I closed my notebook, hoping to get away before Prader showed up. He had a way of pushing interns, sometimes even medical students, into areas that were really the resident's responsibilities. I had had enough of that earlier in his office, and I didn't feel like making an afternoon of it too. I was just on the point of leaving the station when he walked on the ward with Berquam. Motioning Berquam on to the conference room, he came into the station.

"Is Dr. McMillan available?" he said.

I said I thought he was at lunch.

"Have him paged. Tell the paging operator he's wanted in the conference room. Immediately."

"Yes, sir."

"I want you there, too. Is Mrs. Berquam here?"

I told him she was in Mary's room, and while I dialed the operator he went to get her. Later, as I followed them down the corridor to the conference room, I could hear the operator paging McMillan over the loudspeakers.

Prader didn't waste any time, but began talking even while we were getting settled. "I wanted to talk to both of you this morning," he said, choosing a chair that faced the Berquams. "Unfortunately, I was called away. I apologize."

Mrs. Berquam glanced at her husband who remained stonily silent. Prader gave me a fleeting look and continued: "As I am sure you are aware, our hospital is a major referral center. In a very real sense then, it is as much a place where the most difficult to manage and potentially dangerous medical situations are continually presenting themselves as it is a high-powered diagnostic center. With the kind of hospital this necessitates, and the type of severely ill patients we receive, actions must be swift and at times begun almost reflexly. I'm sure you understand and appreciate the need for that."

He waited a moment and then went on. "We try to minimize the initial shock of the admission and any confusion that the logistics of the situation may generate, by talking—either myself or one of my staff—with the parents of the newly-admitted child so they know exactly what they can expect, what will be done, the possible complications of the various procedures, and, probably most important, what the diagnosis really means. I am convinced that this kind of initial discussion is important, not only in regard to disorders of the blood, but any chronic disease where there is a likelihood of repeated admissions, clinic visits, continuing therapy, or where the medications themselves may be dangerous or debilitating.

"The neurologists have such discussions for the degenerative brain diseases; the endocrinologists with their new diabetics; the renologists with their renal transplantation candidates. We in hematology make a very special effort in this regard. We believe it is particularly important, with diseases like your daughter's, to discuss what we are up against.

"In this case, Mr. Berquam, with your obvious knowledge of the field, such a discussion would be superfluous." Prader paused to let this sink in. "However," he continued, "I must point out that work is going on, here in our own research laboratories and elsewhere as well, not only to develop better drugs but to give us a better understanding of the disease itself, so that we may find a cure."

Here he turned to Mrs. Berquam who was sitting nervously on the edge of her chair. He had been speaking directly to her husband; now he was attentive to her. "If your daughter has the type of leukemia I think she has, them I'm fairly confident we can stop her disease and clean up her blood. As physicians we can offer her time, perhaps a good deal of time, and a large part of it, we can say from our experience, will be symptom-free."

Mrs. Berquam looked at her husband hopefully. Prader must have seen how stubbornly, if almost imperceptibly, he was shaking his head, but he chose not to notice.

"Tell me, Mr. Berquam," he said, "what would you say about the treatment of a child with cystic fibrosis?"

Berquam was taken back by the direct question. "I don't know about cystic fibrosis," he said. There was an awkward silence as Prader waited for him to go on. "Many of them have anemia," he said, obviously feeling pushed, "but that's all I know."

Prader nodded in agreement. "What you say is true. Unfortunately, the reason for the anemia is that the treatment of their basic disease is at best palliative. For the more severely affected children, however, the prognosis is hopeless."

Berquam stared at him with continued hostility, but he was obviously listening as Prader continued: "It is the same with other chronic diseases. Sickle cell anemia is one that I'm personally familiar with. Those affected by it will have constant pain, constant liver disease, constant kidney destruction, neurological deficits, lung problems, bone problems, and heart failure. They will die well before they are twenty-five, and most of those twenty-five years will be spent in hospitals where we can do nothing but give them IV fluids and send them home between admissions.

"And then, of course, there is multiple sclerosis, amyotrophic lateral sclerosis, metachromatic leucodystrophy; the agammaglobulemias, Aldrich Syndrome, the fatal granulomatosis diseases of childhood, and so on. Believe me when I tell you the world has been lulled into a false sense of medical security, and expectation of medical miracles, of escape from pain and suffering, of sudden cures, all because in one field of medicine—infectious disease—there is the magic bullet of antibiotics. But even in that field we barely keep ahead of disaster by expending millions of dollars of research to keep up a constant infusion of newer and newer antibiotics as the older ones become useless. As for the rest, we are still fumbling around in the dark ages. Today we use prednisone and Imuran with the same lack of knowledge as when we used mustard seed and witch hazel. Most treatments today are still prolonged and painful, and the results for chronic diseases, no matter what they might be, are spotty at best. At the most they—" and here Prader hesitated as if he suddenly realized he'd gone too far, then added quickly, "at the most, they simply give us time.

"Tell me, Mr. Berquam, as a medical professional, what would you do in the case of any chronic disease I've mentioned, where the eventual outcome, no matter what you do, is death?"

"I'm not an expert on chronic diseases," Berquam said.

"Well, I am, and today leukemia is no more terrible than the other diseases I've named. Today in hematology we have drugs that give remissions which specialists dealing with other chronic diseases would give anything to have. A cure may be still a long way off, but eventually we will have a whole armamentarium of drugs on our shelves just like antibiotics, to be used one after another so we can maintain our patients in a constant state of remission."

Mrs. Berquam was watching her husband, her body tense, her face taut with anxiety, while he sat there, chin down, maintaining his stubborn silence.

"What would you think," Prader went on, "of a parent who didn't want his child with sickle cell anemia treated because no matter what we did the child would not live past twenty or twenty-five? Or wouldn't want a pneumonia to be treated in a son with cystic fibrosis because it would not affect the basic disease process and the child would die anyway?" He paused as Berquam glanced at his wife who seemed on the verge of tears.

"Your daughter has a dread and deadly disease. There is no magic bullet. But there is a treatment.

"As I said before, we have a lot to learn and a long way

to go, but we couldn't have got as far as we have without the help of parents like you. We need your help as much as you need ours. All the drugs we have now are effective to some degree, but how much more effective one is than the other, or if it is better to give them all together, or give them every other day, or three days a week, that we don't know. The only way to find out is to use them in various combinations and then compare the results.

"This is where we ask your help. I feel strongly that your daughter should be treated. She is of course *your* daughter, and I can understand your concerns and feelings. But our position, and I don't think it is an unreasonable one, is that we should use what we have struggled so hard and so long to obtain, and at such great expense and suffering, not only for your daughter but for those others who will be coming after her."

Berquam glanced at his wife whose eyes were fixed on him as she wavered between hope and fear.

"What we would like to do," Prader went on, "if you agree, is to use a special protocol of medications for your daughter, where dosages and time of treatment have already been established. Whether the particular group of drugs we use will be more effective, or less, than the other protocols we are using, I don't know. Nor does anyone else. I can guarantee, though, that each drug by itself has proved effective to some degree."

"But in the end," Berquam said, "she'll die anyway. Right?"

"Yes, she will die anyway."

Despite her effort to control herself, Mrs. Berquam's eyes welled with tears.

"And for a large part of whatever time she'll have left she'll be ill," Berquam said. "Right?"

"At the end, yes."

"And the beginning? And the middle?"

"There is that possibility, though our patients usually spend less than ten percent of their survival time hospitalized, and most of that is at the end."

Mrs. Berquam was sobbing openly now. The discussion was a cruel trial for her.

"And the fevers? And the infections?" Berquam demanded. "The bleeding."

"No one can tell how long the remissions will last."

Prader waited. Berquam, shaking his lowered head, was obviously unconvinced, and at the same time painfully aware of his wife's misery. I could feel the tension in the room, like a physical presence as she watched her husband through her tears, mutely pleading with him. At last, with a deep sigh, he reached across and took her hand.

"I don't want our child to suffer,'" he said softly, so softly I could hardly hear him.

"Nor do we," Prader said.

"Very well," Berquam said, almost with a groan, as if consent had been wrenched from his very guts. "We'll do as you say."

If Prader felt anything at the moment—satisfaction at having persuaded Berquam, pity for the parents' anguish, whatever—his face did not show it. "While your daughter is in the hospital," he said, "the house staff will be responsible for her care. That is the policy of the department. They are all competent physicians and they will of course be responsible to me."

It was over. It had been a magnificent performance on Prader's part—no question about that. If it had been any other professor I might have congratulated him, but Prader didn't give me a chance. He didn't even look at me as he walked out.

12

It was only after I left the conference room that I realized McMillan had not shown up despite his being paged. I thought perhaps there had been an emergency, but when I called the paging operator she said McMillan had answered and she'd given him Prader's message.

I asked if he'd had any other pages and she said no. Nor had there been any call from the emergency room. It wasn't like McMillan to ignore a page; worried, I went to look for him. I found him in the lab, going over some urinalyses.

"The operator said you answered the page," I said.

He looked up from the samples. "That's right."

"But you didn't show. Anything wrong? I mean—"

"No," he said. "Nothing's wrong. I just had a lot to do."

"Didn't the operator tell you Prader wanted you in the conference room?"

McMillan shrugged. "I know what has to be done. They're going to let her be treated, aren't they?

"So you see," he said when I nodded, "Prader didn't need me. This place is too busy to be where you're not needed."

"Yeah, but he's not going to see it that way," I said.

"That's his business. Even when I'm not needed I go if I can learn something. But just to sit is not my thing. I don't learn any more from such conferences."

I guess my face must have registered dismay or something, the way McMillan went on trying to explain.

"Look," he said, "they can't do everything. Some professors, I admit are better than others, but all the bosses around here are researchers and/or administrators." He put the test tube he had been holding back in the rack and picked up the one next to it. "That's their interest; that's how they run this place and how they maintain their position and why they're promoted. Talking to patients or parents is not their thing, even if they think it is, or are forced into it. They really don't know how; even if they care, they don't know. Oh, I admit they can get a patient to do things and you can learn all the tricks by listening to the professors, but once you've learned it's silly to keep going back to them.

"Wait a minute," I said defensively, "I've sat in on two of Prader's conferences, and—"

"Don't get me wrong. If something's the matter with your heart you want Professor Brown to find out what it is. And Blanchard to operate on it. You want to listen to everything they have to say about heart disease, and to Prader about hematology. You need them and the patients need them. But being an expert on parts doesn't make you an expert on the whole. Learn all you can. I only wonder if you'll be sitting in on Prader's conferences next year because you're learning something or because you want to keep him on your side.

"Believe me," McMillan added, "no matter how hard you listen, there will still be times around here when you'll be on your own."

A short time later Cranston, one of Prader's research fellows, came by the ward with the protocol for Mary's treatment.

"Dr. Prader wants you to use this protocol," he said, "but since the patient is already on prednisone, he's not going to include her in the study." He handed me the card.

"I'll tell McMillan and start it," I said.

"By the way," Cranston said as he was about to leave, "did anything happen to Prader?"

"What do you mean?"

"Well, this morning he was OK, but when he came back to the lab a little while ago he was out for heads. There was nothing any of us was doing that was right."

"Nothing special happened. He talked to some parents, convinced them to let their daughter be treated. That's all. He really knows his stuff. I tell you, it was something to see."

"Humph!" Cranston snorted. "Maybe he didn't think so."

The protocol called for prednisone—40 milligrams per meter squared per day—and vincristine—1.5 milligrams per meter squared per week. Also included was irradiation to the brain and spinal cord of 1,000 rads over a period of a month.

There were three other protocols Prader could have chosen: the BIKE, VAMP, or POMP programs. The BIKE involved induction of remission with vincristine and prednisone followed by maximum dosages of 6-Mp and cyclopospamide. The VAMP and POMP programs used combinations of several drugs all given at one time, and then used again together to eliminate remaining cells. Prader picked the protocol that was the simplest, had the fewest drugs, and was best tolerated by the patient, the one with the fewest side effects from the drugs themselves.

McMillan wasn't happy with his choice. "As sick as she is," he said, "blastic crisis, bone pain, central nervous system involvement, thrombocytopenia—hell, just prednisone and vincristine are too tame for her."

I must have looked dubious, and even a bit shocked, for he went on hastily: "After all, he's not putting her in the study. He could have picked any program he wanted."

"It's an accepted treatment," I said.

"Sure, but he could have mixed protocols, or chosen one with more meds. And if for whatever reason he's set on prednisone and vincristine, he could still have increased their dosages or administration rates."

"That's what the whole study is for," I said.

"She's not in the study," McMillan reminded me.

"What I mean is nobody knows which drugs are best, that's the reason for the study. The other protocols all have side effects. The kids get sick as hell; their hair falls out, they can't keep any food down, lose weight, can't sleep. You know the rest—nerve damage, loss of sensation, bladder bleeding, infections. Maybe prednisone and vincristine in these dosages are just as good as any of the other schedules, without all the complications from the drugs themselves."

"Maybe," McMillan said. "But the whole idea of leukemic therapy is to kill every cell. Remember? Every cell."

"But no one knows," I protested.

"So you stay with the protocols. That is, you stay when you have to. The final results of the protocol study aren't in and won't be in for a long time yet. It may be four or five years before the follow-ups are completed and the data tabulated. Maybe, as you suggest, prednisone and vincristine will prove to be as effective as the other programs, and I agree we simply have to know and I'm willing to do what has to be done to find out. But the theory, with all its emphasis on cellular resistance, points to the more drugs the better. So until the final results are in, we ought, where we can, to be using everything we've got.

"Everything," he repeated emphatically, stopping me before I could interrupt, and when I tried to go on he would have none of it.

It was the first time McMillan had ever stopped me in the middle of a discussion. The first time he simply refused to go on, or just to listen.

Maybe the reason I was disturbed by his attitude was because secretly I agreed with him that we ought to go all out, use everything we had. There's a kind of security in knowing that no matter what happens you've done all you could—a kind of hedge against defeat. The implication that it was possible to do more was worrisome; it struck at the very heart of how we viewed ourselves as doctors.

On the other hand, the protocol that Prader had sent down was absolutely acceptable; it was being used all over the country. As he told the Berquams, each drug had already proved its own individual effectiveness.

And yet I was bothered. What if McMillan was right? I'd always thought of the study as a necessary tool, a way of establishing the facts, of finally knowing in a totally scientific way what was best. But what if Mary's protocol was not the best, the most effective? Then in a very real sense, concerns for truth and knowledge aside, even the idea of a greater good, we were sentencing her to a death that might have been avoided or at least delayed.

I tried to console myself with the fact that no one really knew what was best, but my concern kept intruding. With no study to hide behind, responsibility suddenly moved up very close. The child was very sick; just maybe we should try to do more. For a while I thought of going to Prader, but dismissed the idea as foolish. At best it would be sheer presumption on my part. What could I say that he didn't already know?

And for the first time I was struck with the realization of what he had to face every day, the decisions he had to make every day, when life and death were the stakes. I had only one Mary to worry about; Prader had hundreds.

III

13

That afternoon we began Mary's vincristine; McMillan and I drew it up ourselves. Usually it was the nurses who prepared the medications, but anti-leukemic therapy we administered ourselves. The drugs were so powerful that you had to be sure the needle was well in the vein, that there was a good back-flow of blood into the syringe, and that you injected at a slow but constant rate or you ran the risk of injecting the drug into the tissues around the vein, injuring the muscles and skin and causing lesions much like third degree burns. You also had to be sure that the precise dosage was delivered; too much could cause severe and at times life-threatening reactions.

The two drugs inhibited leukemic cell production, but at the same time they also interfered with the body's already limited ability to handle infections, so that overwhelming bacterial, viral, and fungal infestations could become as much a problem and concern as the leukemia itself.

McMillan was going over some of the minor complications of vincristine so I'd know what to look for, when Mrs. Berquam appeared. She looked worn and she listened quietly as McMillan told her we were about to treat her daughter. He explained briefly how it would be done and the nature of the drugs. If he still had any reservations about the protocol he gave no sign of it.

The next morning when we were on rounds, Berquam himself came on the ward. He ignored us and went directly to Mary's room.

"Are you going to talk to him about the protocol?" Mrs. Gowan asked.

"We talked to his wife yesterday, didn't we?" Lang said. "How many times do we have to explain the same thing? I mean, parents talk to each other, don't they?"

Mrs. Gowan shook her head but didn't say anything. She just looked at Lang as if maybe he wasn't responsible for what he was saying.

"I'll talk to him after rounds," McMillan said.

By the third day Mary was much improved. We gave her the vincristine after lunch, so it wouldn't interfere with her eating. Chris, who was taking care of Mary, was in the treatment room when I came in to get the drug. Mrs. Gowan tried to keep as much continuity of patient care as she could by assigning each nurse the same primary-care patients each day. Having to rotate her nurses through three shifts, coupled with the number of patients admitted and all the procedures that were done off the ward, made it an almost impossible task. But she insisted that primary-care patients came first, however much this might strain the already over-strained system. At the very least it gave the doctor some idea of which nurse to ask about which child.

I had thought that Chris and I were on good terms, but after the Berquam episode it seemed to me she was keeping pretty much to herself.

The vincristine was in the refrigerator and when I took out the vial she handed me the sterile saline. I calculated the dosage, and using the saline drew out the correct amount.

"McMillan should be doing this," I said. "Berquam doesn't seem to bother him. For me, when he's in the room it's like walking into a lion's den."

"Well," Chris said, "after all—"

"After all, what?"

"Mr. Berquam's not very happy."

"That's obvious."

She looked as if she was about to give me an argument.

"Listen," I said, "he agreed to have her treated, didn't he? All he had to do was say no."

"Oh, really. It's as simple as that, huh? All he had to do was say no."

"Nobody twisted his arm," I said. "He decided himself. OK?"

Chris just shrugged and turned away. As if what I was saying wasn't worth her further attention.

I found Mary sitting up in bed, holding a doll her parents had brought her. She was alert enough to glance at me apprehensively. Mrs. Berquam said hello, but her husband just looked through me.

"This won't take long," I said to her, ignoring her husband. "If you want to wait outside it might be easier."

"Don't go," Mary pleaded, reaching out for her father who had got up from his chair.

"It's alright, dear," Mrs. Berquam said. "We'll be right outside."

"It's not going to hurt," I told Mary. "I think I can inject it right into the IV tubing and not have to stick you."

She looked unconvinced.

"Honest. I won't stick you unless I have to."

Berquam brushed past me as if I wasn't there, and followed his wife out of the room.

I was able to use the IV. The injections took no time at all.

"There you are, Mary. That wasn't so terrible, was it?" She gave me a small, impish smile. "It's not all bad here. And it will get better, I promise."

We forgot about the Berquams after that, what with other problems and concerns. There is a pressure in referral and training centers for visible results, an overall expectation that things will be done and done and done until they are accomplished. Professors get promoted by producing; medical students get recommendations by accomplishing; interns maintain their image by getting things done. You are after results, and once you get them you move on. Personal interactions between doctor and patient might be desirable, but the pressure is to get the patient treated, make the diagnosis, correct the problem, get the lab value normal, cure the disease. So we concentrate on the heart, or the lung, instead of on the human being, not because it is easier but because it is expected; we have to.

Mary continued to improve. Her bone pain gradually disappeared and after a few days her mother was able to wheel her up and down the corridor. Prader came by at least once every other day. He was pleased with the way things were going and told Mrs. Berquam he wanted to get Mary home as soon as he could and follow her in the out-patient clinic.

Berquam would come by at night. He would sit in his daughter's room until visiting time was over and sometimes—at her urging, I suspected—he would wheel her into the corridor. Although Mary was obviously improving, he seemed even more withdrawn than before.

McMillan tried to talk to him mostly about clinical things—lab tests, drug dosages, and the like—but it was more an exchange of data than conversation. Berquam made no effort to hide his hostility. You had the feeling, when he was in the corridor, that he was always watching you, disapproving of what was going on. Rolling Mary up and down the hallway he would slow down to listen for a moment to a conversation coming out of a room, or an argument between two aides. Once, as I came out of the conference room after interviewing the parents of a new admission, I found him standing by the half-open door. He made no answer when I spoke to him, simply moved on.

Although he ignored McMillan and myself and disregarded the nurses, he was not averse to speaking to the parents of other children on the ward; in fact Freddy's father and he seemed to have become friends. At least they seemed to be spending a lot of time together.

The transplant surgeons called Freddy's case a success, and in the sense that he was still alive, it was. But a hospital record of seven huge volumes, not counting laboratory results, showed the price.

"Have you seen his chart?" Lang said. "Christ, it took me over a day and a half just to go through it!"

McMillan had made him go through it all. "You're his doctor now," he said. "Do you want to rely on what others thought, or do you want to be sure and do it yourself?"

Lang didn't have to go over the whole chart to know what was wrong with Freddy. His latest transplant—the kidney from his mother—like the cadaver one before, was rejecting, and because of the rejection he was slowly going into hypertensive renal failure. In all probability, if his blood pressure, even on anti-hypertensive medications, went much higher, the transplant would have to be taken out.

Lang could have started Freddy's history right from the beginning of this latest rejection, from the first day of his fever three weeks before, but McMillan insisted he study the entire chart and he did.

"Here, look at this," he said, throwing his summary down in front of me. "Five pages just dates, operations, complications, medications, and therapy, nothing else."

Yes, it was all there—everything that Berquam must

have feared for his daughter. If I knew then what I know now I'd have realized those pages contained everything any parent of a chronically ill child would fear.

The Handelmans were understandably unhappy when the cadaver kidney the surgeons had used for the first transplant failed. The anti-rejection therapy produced more complications—infections, bone problems, blotted face, fluid retention, vomiting. The kidney, eventually a rotting piece of tissue, had to be removed.

The parents' hopes rose again when the second transplant, the mother's kidney, seemed to be taking. After a year of almost constant hospitalization it looked as if Freddy might finally be able to lead a decent life at home. Now it was all up in the air again and they were back where they'd started.

The Handelmans were feeling pretty desperate, Lang said, after he had interviewed them and taken the history covering what had happened since Freddy's last admission.

"What did you expect?" McMillan said.

"You want to talk to them?" Lang asked. "They're still in the conference room."

"Yeah." McMillan got up to leave. "Any other prospective donors? I mean any of the other relatives been typed?"

Lang looked stunned. "You're kidding. They were chewing my head off about this latest failure. I wasn't about to mention starting the whole thing again. Jesus!"

"Somebody has to. If this one fails, he's going to need another. The sooner they're told, the better."

"Let the surgeons tell them then," Lang said.

"OK," McMillan said. "We'll wait. But somebody's going

to have to tell them, and this admission *you're* the doctor."

Lang didn't look too convinced. As the pediatric house staff on 402 we ran the ward and wrote the orders, but on the surgical patients—those children admitted to pediatrics only because of their age but for surgical procedures—we really acted as consultants. While we watched what the surgeons did and could complain or make trouble about what they decided to do, even cancel an operation if the child had a cold, or a rash, it was still they who made the major decisions. The Handelmans had been around long enough to know it, too.

It took a few days for all the tests on Freddy to come back. Meanwhile I could not help noticing Berquam and Handelman talking seriously during the evenings I was on, and cutting their exchange short if I happened to be passing by. I didn't know why this irritated me so, but it did. Why I should feel they were talking behind my back.

All Freddy's tests—the arterial studies, the kidney function tests, the renal scan and the radioactive washouts—pointed to rejection. At the same time Lang was having real trouble keeping the child's blood pressure under control. Even with massive dosages of Aldomet, Diuril, Aldactone, guanethidine, Minoxidil, and propranolol, his diastolic was still averaging 120. In fact, the dosages were getting so high that Freddy was becoming more and more lethargic from the medications building up in his bloodstream.

A biopsy of the kidney was called for, to be absolutely sure it was rejection and not something else like an occult infection, an obstruction, or even the more remote possibility of acute tubular necrosis. The parents balked at the idea. Lang had mentioned it to them and they demanded to know why, if all the tests showed rejection, their son had to be subjected to a biopsy. He tried to explain, on two occasions, but they kept pushing him on finer and finer points and finally insisted on questioning the surgeons who had suggested the biopsy in the first place.

"They're getting pretty stiff-necked," Lang said. "Do you suppose Berquam's behind it? I mean after all, the morose sonofabitch works in a hospital. He's been getting mighty chummy with Freddy's father. I've even seen the two of them leaving here together."

"So what?" McMillan said. "Don't worry about it. Just do your work. Besides, what can Berquam tell the Handelmans? They know more about transplants than he does. Just spend more time with them yourself, and make sure they know what's going on."

It wasn't that easy, though, to forget about Berquam. It was getting so that whenever you wanted Handelman you found Berquam with him. It was plain that Berquam was getting involved with the other parents too, and not in a casual way, either. As a rule, parents mingled almost aimlessly, but with Berquam in the picture what had been casual encounters seemed to become meetings. More than once as I approached these meetings I experienced the same sudden embarrassing silence. I began to wonder why I was feeling so suspicious.

As Freddy's condition worsened and he went more and more into renal failure, the Handelmans became increasingly hostile. In a sense, they simply stopped going along with us, making us justify every little thing we did or wanted to do, even to the point of questioning the routine things like daily hematocrits and electrolytes. Why did we have to draw blood every day? Why did the nurse have to wake him up last night just to take his blood pressure? Why do you have to repeat that test? What did that potassium level mean? Why another scan? Until Lang was fairly going nuts explaining and reexplaining. But when they started asking highly technical questions, about things like the dosages of ALG we were using, for instance, and peripheral vein renin levels, he really got hot under the collar.

"For Chrissake," he complained, "somebody's feeding them that kind of technical information. How the hell would they know that the Mayo clinic is using half the ALG dose we are. I'm telling you, McMillan, it's Berquam. He's the only one who could be doing it, and you've got to stop him."

We were on afternoon rounds. McMillan looked questioningly at Mrs. Gowan.

"We can't stop them from talking," she said. "At least, I can't."

McMillan said he would talk to the Handelmans the next day, and it seemed to quiet things for a while. But then Freddy had a seizure and we had to call them in at three o'clock in the morning because we thought he might die.

We were faced with the problem of any high-powered teaching and training center—continuity of care. Dr. Kadden was head of the transplant service. He did the surgery or supervised it. But as head of the department and an international authority on transplantation, he was hardly ever around for the more routine things. He left the daily care to his residents and they were forever changing, so that there were times when even we weren't sure whom to call. It was only natural that parents sometimes found the situation confusing.

Cane was the chief resident of the transplant service the night when Freddy had his seizure. He came over, in his surgical greens, as soon as we called, but by the time he got to the ward we had already stopped the seizure. The child was very sick and close to arresting. We had had to do a cut-down, and the room was a mess of tubes, gauze, and emergency equipment.

"Looks bad," Cane said. "His blood pressure still up?"

"Yeah. He might have bled into the brain," I said.

"No question, well have to take out his kidney tonight. Are his parents here to sign the consent?"

"They're on their way."

The Handelmans wanted Kadden. In the middle of the night, with nurses, aides, doctors, and technicians running in and out of the room, tubing and catheters all over the place, their son unconscious and connected to monitors clicking and flashing all around him, they wanted the chief.

Cane tried to talk to them. "I know how you feel," he said, "but Dr. Kadden is out of town at a conference."

"Then what about Dr. Simpson?" Handelman asked.

"He's no longer on this service. I'm responsible—"

They knew Cane was the new chief resident, but they still wanted Kadden.

"He's not here," Cane said again.

"Then get him," Handelman demanded.

Cane kept his cool. "Look," he said, "time is important. Your son's already had one hypertension seizure. The medications aren't helping him. If we don't act promptly he may have another and end up severely brain damaged—or dead. I'll try to get hold of Dr. Kadden, but in any case the kidney will have to come out tonight."

Cane couldn't reach Kadden. He called Singleton, one of the staff surgeons, and after explaining the situation to him handed the receiver to Handelman who proceeded to complain bitterly about the lack of concern and the shifting of responsibility. When he saw there was no real choice, Handelman finally and reluctantly signed the operative consent, and with that signature he agreed, as he must have known, not only to the removal of the kidney but to beginning the ordeal all over again, since it would be impossible for his son to live without a kidney.

Half an hour later they were wheeling Freddy out of his room to the OR.

14

Freddy survived. After the operation, Cane, still in his scrub suit, went to talk to the parents while McMillan and I accompanied the patient to the recovery room, wrote the pediatric post-op orders, made sure the nurses understood what we wanted and that all the cut-downs were working well. The whole thing wasn't over and settled until it was almost day. Yet when Mrs. Berquam appeared a little after nine she already knew what had happened. Even before she had seen her own daughter she stopped me in the corridor to ask how Freddy was doing.

In the course of the morning several of the other mothers, obviously informed about the surgery, also questioned me. Mrs. Birkell, whose daughter had been admitted only two days before for a tonsillectomy, even asked specifically if Dr. Kadden was back in town. When I told her I didn't think so, she asked me if he had been reached.

"I don't know," I said. "Why?"

"Oh nothing." She shrugged off my question.

"No, tell me," I said, "I'd like to hear. Do you know the Handelmans?"

"Not really."

"Believe me, Mrs. Birkell," I said, trying to reassure her, and at the same time resenting her defensive attitude, "the operation had to be performed. There was no other choice."

"But Dr. Kadden was their doctor, wasn't he?"

"Yes, in a way, as the head of the transplantation service."

"He did put in the last kidney, didn't he? I mean he did the last operation. Don't you think he should have been there? After all, the child was his patient. It was his operation that failed."

I was taken aback that she thought the head of the department of the largest transplant unit in the country had to be immediately on hand, especially for anything as simple as removing a kidney.

"He's a busy man," I said impatiently. "He can't always be present. He teaches, he travels, he lectures. Emergencies are bound to occur, and if he's not around, things still have to be done. It's not as if he leaves his patients unattended, you know. The doctors under him are superb surgeons. They go right from his program to professorships at other centers. I assure you those who operated last night were thoroughly competent."

"Still, he should have been called," Mrs. Birkell insisted.

"Perhaps," I said, backing off. What was it to her that Kadden hadn't been called, I wondered.

Then I learned from Lang that one of the other mothers had quizzed him if Kadden had agreed to the emergency procedures.

"She wanted to know if he'd been consulted," Lang said. "Hell, I was surprised she even knew who he was."

"How about the others?" I asked. "Did anybody else ask you what happened last night?"

Lang nodded.

"Doesn't it bother you? I mean all of a sudden everybody getting so concerned about what's going on with one patient?"

"No," Lang said. "Not particularly. Gossip is always with us. An operation in the middle of the night is an interesting event."

"I don't mind the questions," I said. "It's the way they're asked. As if we were all being put on the spot."

The Handelmans had stayed through the rest of the night, waiting near the recovery room. Mrs. Handelman left in the morning, and then only at McMillan's and Cane's urging, and perhaps because she had to get her other children ready for school. Her husband stayed on, and when in the afternoon the surgeons transferred Freddy back to 402 he stayed with him until the child was settled in and beginning to wake up. None of the parents who had questioned Lang and myself spoke to him. For all their seeming earlier concern, they acted as if nothing had happened.

We had two emergency admissions that morning one after the other. The first was a newborn infant in massive heart failure from a congenital heart defect. The other, admitted at almost the same time, was a toddler with encephalitis and liver failure.

As soon as they reached the ward we had them in the treatment room, side by side on separate tables. I did the cut-down on the newborn, while Lang started on the toddler. Standing between the tables McMillan directed us, helping where he had to. Mrs. Gowan ran the nurses, cracking open vials of medicine, drawing up the drugs, assisting where she could.

The baby was cold, his skin a mottled sickly gray. Even with Mrs. Gowan holding the oxygen mask over his face, he was struggling to breathe, his little chest moving in pathetic exhausted heaves. Every now and then while I was working I heard McMillan beside me asking for something—a new needle, a syringe, some Apresoline, but I was too busy to look up. Within five minutes I had the cut-down in and had pushed in the first dose of digitalis and diuretic. I stopped only to let the portable chest film be taken and then moved back in again.

While I was putting in the central venous pressure, McMillan had called the cardiologist and on the basis of the X ray it was decided to do an emergency heart cath. Meanwhile the neurologist who had come up to help Lang told him that his patient would have to have an exchange transfusion. By now there were so many doctors and nurses in the room you could hardly move. While they were setting up the cath lab I went out with McMillan to talk to the baby's father who had ridden to the hospital in the ambulance with him: the mother was still in the hospital recovering from the delivery.

We took a quick history about the delivery or rather what he knew about it, explained what we felt was wrong and what had to be done, and got permission for the heart cath. The child did not survive the catheterization procedure; he died on the table.

It took a while to explain to the father that the heart defect would have been inoperable even if the child had not died during the catheterization, that the trouble was not due to a genetic defect but was simply an abnormality of organ development. We explained there was no reason to believe that their future children would be at any greater risk with regard to heart defect than any other child being born. We arranged for the autopsy permission and had him sign the forms.

It's hard to tell a parent his baby is dead, but the father took it well, at least while we talked to him. It was not until later, much later, it struck me that neither McMillan nor I had asked him how he felt, or about his wife and how he thought she would take the unhappy news. All we had done was give him the medical facts.

We were not very good with death. Indeed, death was something rarely mentioned on the ward, or any ward for that matter. In a world of dying, death was the really unacceptable thought.

By the time we got to the treatment room, the other patient was already being transfused. "It looks like a Reye's syndrome," Lang said. "At least his blood glucose is eight, and his liver function tests are really screwed up. His SGOT is 7,000. The neurologist agrees."

"You've got to be sure," McMillan cautioned. "You'll have to do a spinal tap."

We had three more children admitted that afternoon. The last one needed tomograms so that it was well into the evening before I got back to 402. The ward was quiet. A few of the parents not sitting in the rooms were in the auditorium with their children watching television. I was surprised to see the light on in the conference room. We liked to keep that room available for emergencies, a place to put parents while we were working on their child. There was no place else on the ward that was private; if we didn't want to use the patients' rooms, the conference room was all we had.

I went to ask whoever was using it to leave, and was about to walk in when I heard Berquam's voice and saw the back of his head through the partly open door.

"Believe me, Herb," he was saying, "I've been around hospitals long enough to know they could have got Kadden for you if they'd wanted to. How hard do you think Cane tried? If you were a bank president or the head of some big company, you can bet they would have let Kadden know. Hell, Kadden would have chewed Cane's ass if they had done a major procedure on an important person without first getting his permission."

"He was out of town," Handelman said.

"It's been eighteen hours since. Have you heard from him yet? There is absolutely no reason why you should have to deal with anybody but the boss, especially with doctors—residents you've never seen before. He's your child, not theirs.

"And the money! Where the hell are you going to get the money? Those guys you talked with last night, are they going to give it to you? Think they even take the expense into consideration? Just sitting here's a hundred and seventy-five dollars a day. And what about another transplant with the additional surgical and intensive care charges? Anybody ask how you're going to pay for all that? Anybody even care? What about the rest of your family? How are they going to live? You've got to learn to take care of yourself, Herb.

"I'll bet nobody's mentioned home dialysis to you, have they? It's not because they don't know about it. It's because the experts in home dialysis aren't here; they're up in Boston. They're pushing their own things down here and you pay the price. The patients always have to pay the price. Kadden's thing is recipient typing and transplantation, not dialysis. If you were in Boston they'd be talking dialysis, not transplantation. Each specialist pushes his own thing, tears down the other guy's ideas while he minimizes the risks and complications of his own. The patient be damned."

I couldn't believe my ears. I just stood there coming to a slow boil as Berquam continued his harangue.

"Why do you suppose the Krugers are using that expensive antibiotic, instead of a less expensive one? I'll tell you why. It's because the damn urologists don't even know how much the drugs cost that they prescribe. That kind of knowledge isn't part of their work-up. Or take the Hartmans. Having to have that skin biopsy on Friday instead of the following Monday, with a weekend of sitting around doing nothing at a hundred and forty a day? Or those iron pills the intern gave Joan Birkell to take, just to see if they worked.

"Look, Herb, I've been around hospitals a long time. I've seen enough wrong diagnoses, wrong treatment, wrong medications. Weeks and months of pain because people were afraid to question their doctors. Doctors don't like being challenged or told they're wrong or even being questioned—about anything. It's a closed shop. Hell, we have an obstetrician at our hospital who induces all his labors and has a higher incidence of brain-damaged newborns than any other obstetrician in the area. They all know about it. The nurses talk and make sure that none of their friends go to him, but he's still practicing and making a fortune. Nobody stops him. Believe me, Herb, I know doctors, and a more self-assured, self-righteous lot you've never seen—"

Enough, I thought, I've had enough. Goddamned troublemaker. That's the thanks we get for saving his daughter's life.

In the doctors' station Chris was bringing the vital-signs chart up to date.

"Have you seen McMillan?" I asked angrily. I must have sounded strange, the way she looked at me. I was really burned up.

"He's not on tonight," she said.

"Do you have his phone number?"

"It's in the top drawer, over there." She pointed to the admitting desk. "What's wrong? One of the patients?"

"No, one of the grateful parents."

"Mr. Berquam?"

"Right the first time. Bastard's working Handelman over."

"Why bother Dr. McMillan?"

"You want another parent trying to check his child out against medical advice? This kind of thing is best stopped at the outset."

"What kind of thing?"

"Why the hell don't you go over to the conference room and listen for yourself?" I said.

"I have," Chris said, as cool as I was hot.

"You have? What do you mean you have?"

"I've heard him talking to other parents."

"Like that? You mean—"

"Like what?"

"Like scaring Handelman. Like telling him we're not competent and he'd better check up on everything we're doing."

"I don't think he's saying that."

"You don't, eh? Then for Chrissake go listen yourself."

"Maybe you're the one should go back and listen," Chris said stiffly, and walked out of the station.

I wasn't used to having a nurse walk out on me like that. My hand shook as I dialed McMillan's number.

"Sorry to bother you," I said. "There's something going on here you should know about." I told him what I'd overheard.

"Yeah, OK," McMillan said. "Handelman still there?"

I guess I knew when I called him he'd come in. I felt relieved when he said he would.

He came on the ward about fifteen minutes later, wearing wash pants and a blue shirt open at the neck, and looking thoroughly bushed.

"Sorry," I said. "I suppose it could have waited. But—"

McMillan shrugged. "What about Freddy."

"Stable. Blood pressure's OK and he looks like a rose. We'll be able to cut back his dialysis to twice a week instead of every other day—What are you going to say to him?"

"Which one, Handelman or Berquam?"

"Christ! I wasn't even thinking of Berquam. He's like a lost cause. I mean Handelman."

McMillan puffed out his cheeks. "I'll tell him what he already knows. This isn't a perfect place, but it's the best available, and as far as medicine goes, there's none better." He paused, frowning, as if trying to recall something that had slipped his memory. "Where is he?"

"I saw him go into his son's room just before you came in."

McMillan nodded and left the station. I finished the last of the progress notes and was about to leave when I saw Chris standing near the medication cart in front of Mary's room, talking to Berquam. It bothered me to see them talking in such a friendly way, and I was aware of my annoyance as I went to check two kids who had spiked fevers earlier in the evening. When I came out Chris was pushing the med cart down the corridor to the next set of rooms. I stopped her.

"Look," I said, "I need to know what's going on around here. Anything that affects patient care is—"

She started to push the cart but I stopped her again.

"Come on. I saw you talking to Berquam just now. Fine. It's a free country. You can do what you want. All I want to know is what he's up to. What's he planning to do next?"

Chris looked at me as if she thought I might be slightly paranoid. "He's not planning anything," she said.

"So he's not planning. Then just tell me whom he's going after next. I don't like calling McMillan in on his night off for something like this. Once is enough."

"I told you he's not going after anybody."

"Oh, no? I don't know if he hates all doctors or just us, and I don't care. But I'm not going to have another patient submitted to what Handelman just went through."

"What Handelman *just* went through," Chris said scornfully. "Excuse me, I've got to pass my meds."

I grabbed the cart. "No games, damn it. This is—"

But at that moment Berquam came out of his daughter's room. His sudden appearance, not more than five feet away from me, put an end to our conversation. He was the last person I wanted to talk to and I went on my way.

McMillan must have finished talking to Handelman while I was busy with a new emergency admission, because I didn't see him leave. The child was an asthmatic in respiratory failure and he kept me in the treatment room most of the rest of the night.

15

The next morning the picture was brighter. Freddy was cheerful. The Reye's syndrome had stopped seizing and it looked as if his liver wasn't as badly damaged as we had thought. The two children with dehydration were ready to go home, the asthmatic child was breathing better, all the surgical patients were stable, and no one seemed to be infected.

When we came into Mary's room we found her perched on top of the bed covers with her legs folded under her, playing with a picture puzzle. Despite McMillan's concern about what he considered the inadequacy of her drugs, she had been improving for days and was becoming everybody's favorite, mine especially. The wispiness that had seemed so fragile, so alarming when she was desperately ill hadn't disappeared, but had become a kind of delicateness that was all the more disarming because it was so open and appealing.

"Hello," she said, scanning our faces one by one as we filed into her room, quickly, precisely, as if she was checking us off a boarding list. Apparently satisfied we were all there, she began picking up the pieces of the puzzle to clear the bed.

"No, no, it's alright," McMillan said. "We're just here to say hello. No examination."

She nodded, and just as quickly began putting the pieces back in place. She was wearing a light blue flannel nightgown with a frilly collar, every bow neatly tied. Her hair, parted precisely down the middle and pulled back tightly into braids, accented her big brown eyes and high cheek bones, and made her look older than she was. Suddenly, without looking up from her puzzle, she asked if she could go home.

"I mean," she added quickly, "when I'm better."

"Sure," McMillan said, "we can get you home."

I watched a small smile curl the corners of her mouth and vanish as quickly as it had appeared. She was so feminine, so engaging.

And so alive. What a fool her father was, I thought.

The following day things didn't go so well. Nothing disastrous, just a lot of confusion and a lot of work. Conditions on the other pediatric wards made it necessary for us to take most of the scheduled hospital admissions.

As I remember it, seven or eight new patients came in that day, and in the midst of having to work all of them up we had two emergencies. There were times when the parents were standing two and three deep in the hallway just waiting to get their children into the rooms or have a history taken.

Our ward was always on the verge of being understaffed; that day pushed us over the line. Lang and I cut our histories to the barest essentials and did the minimum necessary physical examinations. To clear the backlog McMillan even began doing off-service work-ups himself. The nurses were absolutely swamped. We tried to help them by keeping our initial orders to a minimum, but even so the day staff didn't have time for lunch and were still hours behind.

When the shifts changed, Mrs. Gowan, who had been busy all day not only with primary care and keeping up with all the orders, but directing the other nurses as well, had to stay to help the three to eleven staff get the new patients to their rooms, medications passed and charted, and orders transferred to the card index.

Some of the parents among those who had to wait the longest became irritable, as well they might. We tried to calm them by explaining that the situation was abnormal and emergencies simply had to be taken care of first, but there were still some who refused to be pacified and complained openly, stalking back and forth between the rooms and the doctors' station until they were finally taken care of and out of everybody's hair. More than once I saw Mrs. Gowan, in the middle of everything else, having to stop to calm some parent, sometimes the same one several times. Lang, having to do the same thing, began mumbling angrily to himself and my own temper was not exactly under control.

We all had to work well into evening visiting hours. The three of us—Lang, McMillan, and myself—were through about nine o'clock, but the nurses were still catching up. Mrs. Gowan was exhausted. She had been on her feet since six-thirty that morning, so it was no wonder she was beginning to get short with everyone. Then all of a sudden she was standing in front of the nurses' station, glaring at one of the parents, a man named Braden.

"I'm saying that you'll have to leave," she said sharply. "I'm sorry, but that's the hospital rules."

"Fifteen goddamn minutes ain't going to break the system," Braden answered angrily.

"There are thirty-seven other children on this floor who would like their visitors to stay an extra fifteen minutes. The rules—"

"To hell with your rules," Braden exploded. "I had to work late tonight and I just got here. I want more time with my son."

"I'm very busy," Mrs. Gowan said coldly. "If you have any complaints you can submit them on paper to the hospital administrator or the medical director. But right now you'll have to leave."

"*You* write the complaint," Braden snapped, his face flushed. 'I'm staying. God knows I'm paying enough for the privilege."

All the while they were arguing, parents and visitors

were passing by on their way out of the ward. Some slowed to listen; others, embarrassed, pretended that nothing was happening.

"He's my child," Braden continued, wagging his finger at Mrs. Gowan. "Just remember that."

She remained silent, biting her lips, taken aback not so much by what Braden was saying as the threatening way he said it. She looked relieved to see McMillan approaching.

"More of your Mr. Berquam's doing," I said to Chris who happened to be standing nearby. "Let him keep on and the whole place'll go to shit."

And in a way it did—or seemed to, at the time. It was as if the ward had become unbalanced. We all felt it in little ways, little requests and demands, even looks that before we would have dismissed or ignored, that we probably wouldn't even have noticed, now suddenly became important. The whole tone seemed changed. No one knew how many parents were involved, how many were really pushing us. Probably just a few. But we were so unfamiliar with any kind of abuse, so used to having others do what we ordered, to expecting our requests and decisions to be adhered to without exception and without discussion, it began to seem like everyone.

Even Lang, who had always made favorites of certain parents, spending more time with them, talking more, gave that up and began treating everybody the same.

"When I'm off this damn ward," he said, "I'll go back to being my usual charming self."

The thing that broke everything open was what happened to Mary.

16

Mary's white count had been normal for days. Her bone pain had disappeared, her liver and spleen had shrunk back to normal size, her eyes were clear and bright.

Prader saw her only twice a week now, on his formal hematology rounds. Since she was my patient I presented her case to his group during rounds, beginning each time with her newest lab values and then going on to her hospital course. Everyone seemed pleased with our increasing success, everyone except Prader who expressed neither pleasure nor displeasure, said nothing in fact, only listened expressionless each time I presented the case. With Mary's lab values normal for over a week and her magnificent clinical responses, some of his research fellows allowed themselves to speculate on the possible length of her remission.

"The average remission in Konster's series was about eighteen months," Kramer said.

"But that," someone offered, "was with radiation to the central nervous system."

"She had central nervous system involvement didn't she?" said another.

"True," Kramer answered, "but it wasn't due to leukemic infiltration."

"Yes, but according to the Bellevue study—"

"That will be enough," Prader said.

There was a sudden awkward silence. I had never seen him stop a discussion so abruptly. Usually if he wanted to change the subject he would simply ask an impossible question.

"Next case, please," he said now, matter-of-factly.

I began cutting down the number of times I examined Mary and even rewrote the orders for her vital signs so that she could sleep through the night without being waked. All evidence of her disease was gone, apparently wiped out.

I took to stopping by just to visit. Initially I had treated her as a child, but she would have none of that. When I learned to treat her as she thought she should be, we became good friends, or rather I should say she permitted me to become her friend. Mary was indeed something special. No matter how hard I was working or how tired I might be, walking into her room was like walking into springtime. She loved to read. Curled up on her bed she devoured the books her parents brought her by the armful from the library.

She was a collector, too. "Before I was sick I used to

collect everything," she said. "I had a lot of bugs. People are afraid of bugs, but I wasn't. I'd keep them for a while and then let them go. I used to collect rocks, too, but it was too much trouble lugging them around." She was thoughtful for a moment and then, as if she were dismissing the whole thing, she added: "But I guess I'm getting too big for that sort of thing now."

One day in the midst of telling me how to cast on in knitting she suddenly stopped to ask: "Do other girls get sick like me?"

"Yes," I said, "some."

"Does it hurt them too."

"Yes," I said, "for a while."

She nodded knowingly and went back to showing me how to knit.

We were pretty self-satisfied with our success with Mary; indeed, we were even casual about it. The fact that daily we were giving her potentially dangerous drugs was of course recognized but it was played down. In the same way the fact that all we were doing as her doctors was injecting chemicals into her body, and it was the drugs that were clearing her bloodstream, was ignored or minimized in our shared achievement of a normal white count.

We were programmed for success. All through medical school we had been told about the wonders of medicine, the triumphs of surgery. The complications, the price paid for each advance, the "trade-offs," were acknowledged but somehow they were never presented to us with the same emphasis as the accomplishments. If our professors had any reservations about certain medications or procedures, these seemed to fade away in the course of their lectures; certainly they were not stressed. We left school buoyed with the idea of success, indeed expecting it as part of medicine. In a world of medical miracles, failures were aberrations and in a way became the patient's fault, not ours, who had after all done all we could. Which explains, I suppose, why we were not so much ill at ease as taken by surprise when a miracle failed.

Our miracle began to fail some two and a half weeks after it began.

I remember, it was after our morning X-ray conference. Every day, from nine-fifteen to nine-forty-five, the whole pediatric house staff would gather in the X-ray department to go over the previous day's films with the pediatric radiologists. On this particular morning McMillan was questioning the radiologist's reading of a chest film on a new cardiac that had been read as negative but which showed hazy areas near the heart. Pushed by our clinical data the radiologist finally admitted the haziness could be due to an infiltrate. At the moment the argument seemed academic since on McMillan's suggestion we had treated the child the night before, but McMillan didn't want a negative report on the chart if the film was in fact positive, even minimally positive.

They were discussing another film when I left to go back to the ward to do a bone marrow I wanted to have down in the lab before lunch. I was in the doctors' station filling out the lab slips for the test, and labeling the tubes with the child's name and hospital number when Chris came in.

She waited until I had finished stamping the last slip before she spoke.

"Mary's complaining of a headache," she said. "I thought you should know."

"We just saw her this morning on rounds," I said. "She looked fine."

"Well, she's complaining now."

I found Mrs. Berquam in Mary's room. She was bent over the bed, anxiously stroking her daughter's forehead. As I came in she looked up at me. I could see she was frightened and I tried to reassure her.

"We checked Mary this morning before you got here, and she was OK," I said. "There's a lot of flu and stuff going around, you know."

Mary watched me as I walked around to the other side of the bed. The sparkle was gone from her eyes. She looked tired.

"She was fine until only a little while ago," Mrs. Berquam said, almost apologetically. "I don't understand it. She was doing so well."

"She's still doing well." I thought of asking Mrs. Berquam to leave so I could examine her daughter without her being in the way but she was hanging on to Mary's hand and I didn't want to worry her more. Besides, Mary didn't seem to be in any distress. She wasn't having any trouble breathing, and her color was good.

"How do you feel?" I said.

She frowned. "My head hurts."

"Well, let's see what the trouble is."

I went over her from top to bottom but I couldn't find a thing. Her eyes, ears, nose, and throat were normal. For a moment after she sat up she looked a bit shaky, but that quickly passed. Her mother tried to help her remove her pajama top, but Mary brushed her hand away irritably and pulled it off herself.

Her skin was smooth and cool. I listened to her chest; her lungs were clear.

Now that she was sitting up she seemed more animated. She smiled when I sat her over the edge of the bed with her feet dangling and made her knees jerk despite her trying to stop them.

I asked her to lie down again on her back, and felt her abdomen and listened to her stomach. Then I lifted her head and flexed her neck until her chin rested on her chest. I did it again. "Does it hurt," I asked.

She pouted, thought for a moment, then shook her head.

"Sure?" I bent her head once more. "OK, you can sit up now."

"I can't find anything," I said to Mrs. Berquam who had been hanging on every move I made. I handed Mary her pajama top and she brushed her hair back with both hands and pulled the top carefully over her head.

"How do you feel now?" I asked.

"Good," she said, but I noticed that instead of continuing to sit up she lay back on her pillow. This troubled me; it wasn't like her to be so listless. Still, there was no evidence of infection nor a sign really of anything else physically wrong.

"It's probably the flu," I concluded, patting Mary's leg. "We'll watch her though. Don't worry."

Mrs. Berquam smiled as brightly as she could and went back to stroking Mary's head as I left the room.

"She's dragging," I told Chris. "It could be just a cold, but let's watch her for a while. I'll check her again myself in a few hours."

"Do you want any lab tests?"

"Why don't you ask the hematology tech to come up and get a white count and smear? And a urinalysis and urine culture. I'll write the orders later."

"Mrs. Berquam's very worried," Chris said.

"I know," I said testily. "I'm not blind."

"Did you talk to her?"

"Jesus Christ. I told her exactly what I told you. Satisfied?"

Goddamn! I thought as I walked away. For a nurse who was supposed to be helpful, Chris was sure becoming a pain in the ass.

The truth was I was on edge. I felt that something was wrong but I didn't know what and it bothered me.

At lunch with McMillan I told him about Mary, how she was not as active as she had been and complained that her head hurt. "There's no fever, her white count's normal, hematocrit is stable; her physical exam was absolutely normal. I went over every inch of her. Nothing—not a thing."

"Blood pressure?" McMillan asked.

"Stable. There was nothing I could find."

"Well, just keep going over her. If it's something it'll show up. Better up her vital signs again and tell the nurses to start taking blood pressures every four hours as well as temps."

I was about to go on with my sandwich when I put it back on the plate.

"Yeah?" McMillan said, looking up from his bowl of soup.

"I was just wondering—What do you think of Chris?"

"A good nurse. Why?"

"Oh, nothing."

"Come on, What's bugging you."

"Well, she's been talking with Berquam, and I think she may be getting in with some of the other parents. I don't say she's egging Berquam on, but she's agreeing with him anyway. As for the rest of the parents I don't know, but she's been on me about our not talking with the parents enough."

"She's probably right," McMillan said. "We should talk more."

"Let me know when you find the time," I said.

There was no question McMillan went out of his way to keep parents posted. I'd watched him keeping Berquam informed on every change in his daughter's condition, every fluctuation in her laboratory values, every up and down in her vital signs. And not only Berquam; he did the same for other parents as well. Now, I wonder if that's what he meant by talking to parents, if he wasn't really talking at them instead. I doubted even then if it was what Chris meant.

Anyway, it was almost three hours later before I could get back to Mary. One of our patients, a hemophiliac who had come in two days before because of bleeding into his knee joint, had begun bleeding again. It took most of the afternoon to treat him—pumping hyalin concentrate into his IV, ice-packing his knee, keeping his blood pressure up and the swelling in his knee down.

17

When at last I was able to look in on Mary I found her half-sitting up, using the pillow as a sort of prop to rest against while she read. She was alone.

Putting down her book she watched me come into the room. I thought she looked troubled. There was still nothing I could put my finger on. She didn't look ill, if anything she looked more alert than in the morning, but there was something about her, a kind of uncertainty, a vague unsettled look in her eyes that made me feel apprehensive, like hearing thunder on a clear day.

I glanced at the day sheet. Her vital signs were normal, and when I asked her how she felt she said again she felt fine.

"Come here." I pulled her closer to the edge of the bed and cupped her chin in my hand. "Anything hurt?"

She shook her head. But the look was definitely there, right under the surface, behind the eyes.

"Mary, tell me," I said, almost pleading for a clue, "is there anything wrong? Something bothering you? Your stomach, or your eyes, your ears?"

She shook her head again.

"Sure?"

"Sure."

"Could you stand up, here by the side of the bed?"

She swung her feet over the edge and jumped to the floor.

"Dizzy?"

"No." She had no hips and her pajama bottoms began slipping down. She quickly yanked them up, untied the draw string and pulling it tighter retied it, then studiously went about making a bow of the string. I offered to help.

"Never mind," she said, "I'll do it."

When she had finished and her pajamas were adjusted to her satisfaction she looked up at me. "Do many people die here?" she asked.

Her question was so unexpected, her gaze so demanding, I just stood there, not knowing what to say.

"Well?" she said impatiently.

"Why do you ask?"

"Daddy says it's better if you die at home. He says doctors only care about what other doctors think—I heard Daddy say it," she added as if that answered in advance any objection I might make.

"Well, daddies can be—" I caught myself short. "What do you think dying means?" I asked.

"They put you in the ground."

"No, no," I said quickly. "You go to heaven. It's sort of nice."

Mary lowered her eyes as if she felt embarrassed for me, and indeed as soon as I had spoken I felt how foolish I sounded, even to myself—foolish and false—and angry at my incapacity to answer this child as simply and directly as she questioned me. I was in fact totally unprepared for what she asked and it was not too surprising. Not once during medical school or during my internship had anyone —professor or instructor—discussed the dying patient, except to indicate what to do for a failing heart, or falling blood pressure. In the whole time I had been responsible for patients there had not been a single scheduled conference, or informal discussion, not one comment on the difference between a ten year old dying and a dying toddler, or how we might as physicians help make our patients' dying less terrifying, less lonely, or even, for that matter how we might feel about death ourselves. We were simply left on our own, and we did not do very well. At times, I think, we made things worse.

"Come," I said now, taking Mary's hand to hide my embarrassment. "A couple of blood pressures and we're finished."

Usually she watched with interest whatever was being done to her. Even when we drew blood she watched to make sure the needle was pointed the right way, the tourniquet placed exactly where it had been before. If we missed the vein she'd wrinkle her little nose and look up at us with such disdain there was no need for her to say anything.

Today her interest was gone. She lay with her eyes

closed paying no attention to what I was doing. As I was unwrapping the last of the cuff, her mother came in. She looked tense and worried.

"She didn't touch her lunch," Mrs. Berquam said.

"You didn't, Mary?" I said.

She turned her head to look at me.

"Did you drink anything?"

"My milk."

"I still think it's a virus, or the flu, I said to Mrs. Berquam. She was standing there so expectantly, I felt obliged to say something, though the truth was I didn't know what was wrong and so I blamed it on a virus. As doctors we had been trained to cater to such expectancy, to give an answer to whatever the question of the moment might be. Actually, I can't remember one of us who ever really admitted to a parent that he didn't know the answer. McMillan came closest, once or twice, but even he hedged and gave the percentages, cited statistics, instead of expressing the concern he must have felt—or just saying he didn't know.

"I'll keep checking her though, just to make sure," I said. "But right now she's OK."

I wrote an order for some blood tests—nothing spectacular, merely a serum sodium and potassium—telling myself it was for a base line, though it was just to do something. I could not get out of my mind that troubled look I had seen on Mary's face when I walked into her room.

Mrs. Berquam must have called her husband at work because an hour later he came on the ward still wearing his own technician's whites. I saw him from the far end of the ward making directly for his daughter's room.

I was on my way to one of our surgical patients, a little boy who had had an abdominal tumor removed three days before and had been hypertensive ever since. We weren't too worried. McMillan had talked with the experts on high blood pressure and tracked down the articles they'd recommended, showing that hypertension was a common result of abdominal surgery and usually disappeared on its own within a week after operative procedure. Still, we kept checking; I agreed with him that even if the high blood pressure was going to disappear eventually we didn't want it to get too high while it was still around.

I was about to begin examining the patient when Mrs. Gowan came into the room to say that Berquam wanted to see me.

"I'm busy," I said. "Get McMillan. He's been dealing with Berquam. Besides, I just got through talking to Mrs. Berquam."

"Dr. McMillan's not around. He went down to the coffee shop."

"Well, he'll be back soon."

"You'd better see Mr. Berquam now," she said firmly.

"She's not feeling well," Berquam said as I came into the room. Mary was asleep, the shades had been drawn, and in the dim light I did not see him at first. He was standing at the far side of the bed, facing his wife.

"She began feeling poorly this morning," I said. "I've already explained to your wife—"

"Explained, explained," Berquam interrupted impatiently. "She didn't eat her lunch, doesn't want her supper.

Her head hurts. What are you doing about it, that's what I want to know."

I didn't like being confronted like this but I made an effort to control myself. "Nothing, at present," I said. "As I told your wife there is nothing to treat yet. I've gone over her, we've ordered lab tests, and—"

"I'm not asking you to find out what's wrong," Berquam broke in. "I already know what's wrong. What I want is for you to make her comfortable. Not tomorrow, or the next day, but now. I want you to give her something now—"

"But—"

"No buts. I don't want any more blood tests. I don't want her to be stuck any more. I don't want you or anybody else waking her up every hour on the hour. I want her to be left alone, and given something for her headache or any other pain she has. Is that clear?"

"Hold it," I warned. "The reason we check her so often, whether you like it or not, is because we don't know what's wrong now—and we have to know what's wrong in order to help her. As for giving her something to make her comfortable—no, wait a minute, let me finish—that might make her feel better for the moment, but it can also keep us from knowing what's wrong until it's too late. Whatever pain medication we give her now could very well mask any real symptoms—Damn it! Will you please just listen —I don't like pain any more than you do. I don't want to see my patients suffer. But I'd rather see them suffer a little than see them dead."

"What the hell is she going to be?" Berquam shouted.

"Now you listen to me, Dr. Wiseguy. You do something and you do it now."

"Robert," Mrs. Berquam pleaded, "please."

His attitude was so threatening and I was so angry we might have come to blows had his voice not wakened Mary.

"Daddy! Daddy!"

Startled, he saw her struggling to sit up—her arms outstretched to him. It was too much; Berquam dashed past me and out the door like a madman.

"It's alright, Mary," I said, trying to keep my voice calm though my heart was pounding. "Daddy'll be back. Just lie down again, honey, and rest." And to Mrs. Berquam, who sat there looking stricken: "I'm sorry," but she seemed not to hear me and I left the room.

Jesus! I thought, we knock ourselves out. To imply we weren't doing our best, that we'd willingly let our patient suffer. I was furious.

I was still simmering when McMillan came back and I told him what had happened. "I think we should call Prader," I said.

"What are you going to tell him?" McMillan said. "That Mary's not feeling well? If we are going to call anybody it should be someone from the infectious disease group."

"It's Berquam I'm thinking about."

McMillan rubbed his chin. "Well," he said, "it's partly our fault. We should have been the ones to tell him about her not feeling well, not his wife."

"Maybe so," I said, not wanting to get into it. "What about Mary? I'm worried."

McMillan said he would check her himself.

"Something's definitely wrong," he said afterward. "Why don't you get some blood cultures? What's the matter, you don't think she needs them?"

"I guess it's a good idea. But to do it right I'll have to stick her five, six times, and her arms are pretty sore already."

"Just get two, then. An hour apart. That should be enough. And a urine culture, just in case. Her electrolytes OK?"

"Sodium's a little down. But not bad."

McMillan was looking at me closely. "You alright?"

"Yeah, I'm alright," I said.

Mary was restless. I drew the last blood culture a little after eight.

"It's just in case," I told Mrs. Berquam. "So we'll know if she's infected. Sometimes, when you're on prednisone and vincristine you can be infected and not know it. These cultures are a way of finding out."

18

Tired as I was, I had trouble sleeping that night. I felt that things were getting out of hand, and I didn't know what to do about it, even where to begin to do something. If parents couldn't see how hard we were working, what we were doing for their children, where had we failed? The sudden tenuousness of our position distressed me. I fell asleep at last thinking how simple it was just to diagnose and treat, and how small a part of the picture it was becoming.

The next morning Mary ate her breakfast and seemed a bit sprier, but I was still worried, not only about her but about her father. I kept expecting more trouble from him, and wondering if I should call Prader. I decided McMillan was probably right. After all, what could I tell Prader? That Berquam wasn't happy? That Mary was uncomfortable? Still, McMillan's not answering Prader's page bothered me, his insistence that we do it all ourselves. Sooner or later we would have to account to Prader.

Mrs. Berquam stayed on the ward the whole day. She was as considerate as always, but she looked more worn and exhausted than ever. I realized later that I should have talked to her. After all, she had spent the evening with her husband; something must have happened, they must at least have talked, and I should have found out what they'd said. But I didn't know how to begin, or maybe even how to handle whatever she might tell me. After lunch I found a half-eaten sandwich, still in its wrapper, under her chair. It was probably the only thing she had eaten all day.

The next day I got a call from bacteriological lab that one of Mary's blood cultures had some growth in it. The blood culture bottles were kept in the bacteriology lab in a large walk-in incubator. I went in with one of the techs. It was warm and humid in the room but not uncomfortable. Mary's two bottles were on the shelf marked 402.

"They don't look bad," I said.

"Hold the first one to the light," the tech said.

The amber fluid towards the bottom of the bottle had the barest haziness to it; the rest was crystal clear.

"The other's OK," she said.

"But if there is growth there's not much here. Right? I said.

"No—But we call any growth positive."

"Did you plate it out?"

"We've subcultured it, but it will take another day or so to grow out."

"Did you smear the subculture and stain it?"

"We do that routinely. It's a gram positive cocci, in chains."

"It could be a contaminate, though," I said hopefully.

She looked at me. "Could be," she said. "There's really not much growth."

"And the other bottle is still negative."

"I'll have more for you when the subcultures grow out. Sorry," she said, "wish I could be more definite."

So do I, I thought, as I went back up to the ward to find McMillan and tell him about the cultures.

"It's probably a contaminate," I said. "I mean its only in one bottle. And there's not much growth."

He thought for a moment, chewing on his lip. "Maybe," he said, "but we can't take any chances. We'll have to treat her."

"That'll mean starting an IV to give her the antibiotics," I said. "If it's a contaminate, she's been sort of crabby all day and having an IV will really bother her."

"And if it's not?" McMillan said. "We'll just start the IV and treat her till we find out—and know for sure. You'd better get some more blood cultures, too, before we start the antibiotics."

"And Berquam?" I said.

"I'll tell him."

I got the culture tray and took it to Mary's room. Mrs. Berquam got up from her chair. Mary looked at me suspiciously.

"You already took today's sample," she said.

"I know; it's like what we talked about, Mary. There are times when we have to do things to keep you feeling well. Now I'd like to talk to your mother for a moment. OK? I'll tell you everything we say."

In the corridor I tried to reassure Mrs. Berquam about what we'd found. "There's only minimal growth in one bottle. If she really had organisms growing in her blood stream they would be in both bottles, and it would be a much heavier growth."

"But where did they come from?" she asked nervously. "I mean the ones in the first bottle."

"Maybe off her skin. Even with all the alcohol we use to sterilize it there could have been one or two organisms that survived and got caught on the needle. Or they might even have been on the stopper of the culture bottle and got carried into the broth when I pushed the needle through the rubber to transfer the blood from the syringe to the medium. It could have been contaminated in any number of ways."

"Sorry, Mary," I said when we came back into the room. "I've got to take a few more cultures."

"No," she protested tearfully, "no more."

"Mary, please, honey," her mother pleaded with her.

"No. No more," she cried.

I asked her mother to leave, but I couldn't calm her myself. For the first time I had to ask someone to come in and help hold her down.

Crying and whining was so unlike Mary, and her mother was so worried about the change in her behavior, I didn't have the heart to mention starting the IV or beginning antibiotics. I took the cultures down to the lab myself and decided to call Prader after all. If anything suddenly broke, I didn't want to have to worry about him, too. Maybe he might even offer some good advice.

When I called from the doctors' station, his secretary answered the phone. She said he was in his lab and I called him there.

"Have you talked to the parents?" he said when I told him about the culture.

I said I had talked to Mrs. Berquam and McMillan was calling Mary's father.

"How do you think they'll take it?" he asked.

"Well," I hesitated, not expecting such a question, "the mother's OK, I think, but I don't know about Mr. Berquam. He can be pretty difficult, as you know. I—"

He cut me short. "What are you planning to do?" he asked.

"I just drew two more cultures. We're going to start an IV and begin antibiotics."

"How sick is she?"

"Well, sir, she's not really that sick. No fever. She's eating alright. But she's a bit cranky. I mean—"

"Which antibiotics?" he asked.

I had just hung up after talking to Prader when Barbara, who was working reliefs, came into the doctors' station and announced that Mary's temperature was 104.

I stared at her in disbelief. "I was with her less than an hour ago," I said. "It was normal."

"Well, it's a hundred and four now."

I told her to call McMillan, and hurried to Mary's room. I found her sitting up but breathing strangely, apprehensively, as if she was afraid that at any moment somebody might suck all the air out of the room and leave nothing for her to breathe.

"How long has she been like this?" I asked her mother.

"Like how?"

"These short little breaths."

"Almost since you left," Mrs. Berquam said. "I thought it was just something that had to do with your drawing her blood. She got so excited. Should I have called somebody?"

"It's alright," I said, to calm her. "I think though it would be better if you waited outside. I want to examine Mary again and it will be easier on her and on you."

"What do you think it is?" she asked, alarmed. "Do you think it's serious?" She was getting up to leave when McMillan came in.

"Mrs. Berquam is going to wait outside," I said.

"Fine," McMillan said pleasantly. "We'll be right out and let you know what's happening."

Barbara, who had just walked into the room, stepped aside to let Mrs. Berquam out.

"Mary," I said, leaning over her bed, "does anything hurt?"

She looked up at me but her eyes were dulled and distant, her drawn face almost expressionless.

So quick! I thought. Jesus!

Barbara pulled back the covers and I saw that Mary's legs were trembling. I took her hand in mine.

"She's clammy," I said to McMillan who had moved to the other side of the bed.

He made to raise her head so the pillow could be removed and she would be lying flat on her back, but he had scarcely lifted it when she grimaced with pain. We exchanged glances. Carefully he moved her head again and this time the pain was so obvious I thought she would scream. McMillan gently laid back her head.

"It takes a while to become evident," he said calmly. "There is a natural course to any illness." He turned to Barbara. "Can you get a spinal tap tray?"

McMillan knew what I was feeling. "You did all you could," he said. "She had no signs. It could just as well have been the flu. All infectious diseases start out the same. Vaguely. Nausea, a rash, coughing, a couple of days of feeling bad. Then the bulging ear drum, pneumonia, or stiff neck. Nobody can fault you. You can't treat until you're sure. Now we know."

My God! I groaned inwardly. Meningitis. As gently as I could I tried to free my hand from Mary's but she wouldn't let go.

I started to ask if we needed a permit, but my voice cracked and I couldn't go on.

It was Barbara who asked the question for me. "Have you got permission for the tap?" she said.

McMillan shook his head.

"But you need one. It's an operative procedure. We had a nurses' conference on permissions and Mrs. Gowan told us to be sure the doctors—"

McMillan cut her short. "I've called Mr. Berquam. He knows his daughter is ill, and that her blood culture may be positive."

"He doesn't know she has meningitis."

"It's a life-threatening situation," McMillan said impatiently.

"Not so loud," I said. "Mrs. Berquam's right outside."
McMillan looked at me. "Come on, will you, let's just get it done."

"Set up the tray," McMillan told Barbara. "I'll talk to her."

"Mary," I whispered when they had left the room. "Mary." I pulled loose my hand. "We're going to have to turn you on your side, and put a little needle into your back. It will be just like a little bee sting, no more. The same kind of needle we use to take blood from your arm. It won't hurt any more than that. Honest."

I thought she heard me but I couldn't be sure. Her face remained expressionless but her lids fluttered open slightly.

"OK," McMillan said when he came back. "Let's get on with it."

When we were ready with the spinal tap I held Mary while McMillan, sitting on a stool by the edge of the sterile-draped bed, pushed the four-inch spinal needle into the small of her back. He worked it slowly through the muscles until finally, with most of its length buried in her back, he slid it between the spines of her vertebrae. When it held up a bit, he changed the angle and shoved.

Wincing, Mary pushed against me and I held her closer.

"It's alright," I whispered. "It's alright. It's over."

I felt Mary relax in my arms and I nodded for McMillan to continue.

Leaving the needle embedded in her back, he carefully pulled out the stylet. The point, fixed in her spinal canal, swung slowly, rhythmically up and down with her breathing. A moment later a thick greenish fluid began bubbling out of the end of the needle.

My God!

"Can you believe that?" McMillan said softly. "Pure pus." He took a sterile test tube from the tray and began collecting the infected fluid as it dripped out of the needle; in all he took out 20 cc's in four separate tubes.

The last few drops were as foul-looking as the first had been. Her spinal canal must have been one sack of pus, infected from top to bottom. It made me sick to think of it. I could feel Mary breathing, could feel her heart beating against mine. A lovely intelligent child, with her whole life still before her, become a culture medium.

McMillan pulled out the needle and threw it into the waste basket. "She OK?" he said.

"Yeah. OK," I said.

He pulled off his gloves and handed me one of the tubes. "I'll start the IV while you take this to the lab and smear it."

"What are you going to use?" I asked.

"Penicillin, Staphcillin, kanamycin—the works. Half right after I start the IV, the rest dripped in over the next twelve hours."

I was relieved not to find Mrs. Berquam in the corridor. I took the tube down to the lab and smeared some of the spinal fluid on a clean slide. It dried almost immediately into thick greenish streaks; I put the slide face up on the staining rack and poured the purple stain over the dried area.

I can remember sitting there in that empty lab waiting

for the stain to work. I felt discouraged and depressed. I was annoyed at myself for being glad Mrs. Berquam hadn't been in the corridor so I didn't have to speak to her, embarrassed at the way I'd handled Mary's question about death, and terribly worried about her condition. I sat alone in that quiet room surrounded by all the equipment of modern medicine, and after four years of medical school and almost a year of internship, of working as hard as it was possible to drive myself, I felt inadequate, inauthentic.

When the slide was ready I shook off the excess stain and put it under the microscope. I found a suitably stained field, and switching to a higher magnification cut down into the thick stain.

"My God!" I cried out loud, as happy as I was surprised.

In the midst of flakes of precipitated stain, cellular debris, and white cells I saw deeply colored purple clumps of cocci—hundreds of them, like great purple kidney beans, filling the field, crisscrossing every millimeter of the microscopic field.

To check I switched to another stained section, and saw the same thing. I had just finished when McMillan walked in.

"Good news, man," I said. "They're pneumococci."

"You sure?" McMillan said.

"They're all over, but they're definitely pneumo. Penicillin should do it. Gives us a fighting chance. Right? That blood culture must have been a contaminate."

I got up to let McMillan have a look. "Yeah," he said. "Incredible. I thought for sure that spinal fluid would be full of pseudomonas, or one of the other resistant organisms. I mean," he said as surprised and pleased as I was, "a child with leukemia on prednisone and vincristine, not to have an antibiotic resistant organism but only a common everyday one like pneumococcus, one sensitive to reasonable doses of penicillin: who would believe it?"

"We might just win this one," I said, all my depression and discouragement dissipated in the euphoria of the moment.

"A better chance, anyway," McMillan said soberly.

I asked about Mrs. Berquam. He told me that after the tap he'd told her what we'd found and she was calling her husband.

Later Barbara explained how he'd obtained the permit from Mrs. Berquam. He had told her that while we thought Mary had meningitis we couldn't be sure until we did the tap, and so she should wait to call her husband until we had the results and would know for sure.

Strange, I thought. After all, we knew Mary had meningitis when we examined her. The only thing the tap told us was the organism.

I expected trouble from Berquam, but there wasn't any. I didn't even know he had come and gone until Barbara told me. When I asked her what had happened, she gave me an offhand answer. She was still peeved about McMillan's arguing with her about the permission. I tried to explain that at some hospitals you didn't need a permission for a tap; it was considered routine procedure, like blood drawing.

"Not here," she said. "You doctors can say the heck with it, but we get the heat. What do you think I'd have heard from Mrs. Gowan in tomorrow's report if there was no permission?"

When I admitted she was probably right she seemed appeased. She said Berquam had stayed only a few minutes. McMillan had told him that Mary had meningitis and had been put on the critical list, but in her case being on critical was more procedural than anything else. Barbara said he'd gone on to tell him that with the organism he'd found as the cause for Mary's meningitis, there was a very good chance the antibiotic would be effective.

"And Berquam?" I said. "He accepted it?"

"No trouble," Barbara said. "None. Dr. McMillan said he just got up and left."

"You sure?" I said.

"I was there," Barbara said.

It still didn't make sense to me. Not as I knew Berquam. Not in view of the situation.

IV

19

About eleven o'clock I checked Mary again. She was sleeping. The nurse's notes said she was rousable, but not much more. The IV taped into her arm was running well.

There was a mild croup admitted from the ER about 1:30 in the morning. The child's chest film was clear and he wasn't in much distress, so I just put him in the mist tent with orders to hydrate him orally through the night.

Chris was the RN on duty. These days Chris and I weren't talking any more than we had to. When I asked her about Mary she said there had been no change, so I went to the snack bar for a coke and then back to my room.

I didn't bother to get undressed. When the phone rang, it was light outside. My watch said quarter to six. Still half asleep I reached for the receiver.

"Yes?" I said.

"This is the aide on 402. The nurse wants you to come right away."

I sat up. "What's wrong?"

"I don't know, Doctor."

"Well, what the hell's the problem?"

"The little girl with meningitis. She's throwing up blood."

The room was a shambles. Chris was holding Mary's head over the side of the bed. Blood and vomit were all over the sheets and the floor.

"I think I got most of it out of her mouth," she said shakingly. "But some of it might have got into her lungs."

Mary's limp body, half on and half off the bed, was tangled up in the sheets. I didn't notice her back until I was close to the bed. What I saw was so startling I just stood there open-mouthed.

The skin on her back and on what I could see of her buttocks once so smooth and delicate had turned a sickening black. Great blue-black welt-like areas ran up and down along her side, as if someone had beaten her with a club. Even as I stood there looking I saw her fingers turning blue and the same color like a stain spreading up her arm.

Chris looked at me uncomprehending, and then I saw terror in her eyes. I pushed her out of the way and jerked Mary's head around so I could see her face. Her mouth fell open and her eyes rolled back. I hit her as hard as I could in the middle of her chest with my fist.

"Get the emergency cart!"

I hit her chest again, then twisted her around on the bed so she was lying flat, and grabbing her chin shoved her head back. For a second I gagged on the sour-sweet smell of vomit. Then I began breathing into her mouth, at the same time keeping my eye on her chest. It didn't move. I could feel the resistance against my own breath.

Frantically I probed her mouth with my fingers, and reaching to the back of her throat pulled out half-digested pieces of food mixed with blood and mucus. Her face and neck, a pasty gray, began breaking out in the same blue-black spots as the lesions on her back and arms. I dug out as much as I could and began breathing into her mouth again.

Come on! Come on! I thought desperately. Come on!

Now her chest moved slightly. Taking great breaths I blew harder and harder in the effort to get more air past whatever was still blocking her airway, until I felt my own heart pounding in my head. I was getting dizzy when Chris crashed open the door with the emergency cart. McMillan was right behind her.

"She's consuming," he said.

Sometimes when there's an overwhelming infection, the organisms in the blood stream start a reaction that causes all the circulating clotting factors suddenly to be used up. With nothing left to stop the bleeding, all the blood vessels and capillaries begin to ooze like a million little cuts.

Leaning over me, McMillan slid his hand up under Mary's pajamas pants. "There's a femoral pulse, but she's clammy."

I was fast running out of breath.

"Here," McMillan said. "Tilt her head back more."

Pushing her chin with my left hand, with my right I

took the laryngoscope he gave me and slipped the blade into Mary's mouth.

"Where's the heparin?" McMillan said. "Is that IV still working?"

The sweat was rolling down my arms as I bent close so I could see along the blade to the vocal cords.

"Give me a clamp. She's obstructed."

Chris put one in my hand. Straining to keep the laryngoscope steady I reached along the blade to pull out more pieces of half-digested food. Squatting as I was, and cramped over, I couldn't hold the scope firm and the blade slipped, digging into the back of Mary's throat. Blood began oozing out of the side of her mouth.

McMillan was listening to her chest. "I can hear it," he said. "Start breathing again."

Now there was no resistance, and her chest moved easily with my breaths. Thankfully I closed my eyes. I heard McMillan say, "Get the bicarbonate," and felt Chris brush by behind me. After every few breaths I had to stop to spit out the blood.

Once I had Mary's airway open it was just a question of doing the right things in the right order. The fact that her heart had probably slowed but never really stopped made things easier. While I continued to breathe for her, to give her the oxygen she needed, McMillan connected her to the cardiac monitor. With its rhythmic beeping filling the room, he gave her bicarbonate IV to correct her acidosis, an ampule of epinephrine and calcium chloride to make her anoxic heart pump more efficiently, and then more heparin. Bit by bit I was able to stop breathing for her. The heparin, too, must have worked; except for a few bluish-purple spots on her forehead, there were no new skin lesions starting up.

It was hardly the right moment for anybody to walk in on us, but looking up I saw Handelman in the doorway. He had started to come into the room, and obviously shocked by what he saw he was leaving in a hurry. It all happened so quickly I seemed to be the only one who saw him, and we were all too busy for me to mention it.

While we were straightening Mary out on the bed the IV infiltrated and we had to put in a cut-down. Even when we cut open her arm to find a new vein she didn't move. We decided we needed a better access in case anything else went wrong, so McMillan put a central venous catheter into her jugular vein.

I held her head as McMillan threaded the catheter down her neck, probing and digging until he found the jugular. Meanwhile Chris was taking blood pressures and drawing up more medications. Twice we had to treat different cardiac arrhythmias, bizarre patterns that showed up on the monitor, and once her blood pressure fell so low that Chris couldn't get a reading. We gave Mary blood then directly into her heart through the central venous catheter and the pressure came up, but dropped again until we gave her more. The X-ray technicians came up and took three series of portable chest films.

It took over two hours, working every minute, to get Mary stabilized, and during all this time she didn't move. But she was breathing and for the present that was enough. She looked bad, limp and unconscious, with tubes running into and out of her body, her skin a mass of blue-black welts. But she was alive. We'd kept her alive. We had used all we'd been taught, all we'd been trained for, and I can remember thinking as I stood by Mary's bed, this is what it's all about.

McMillan was putting another piece of tubing on the IV. "Since she's bled into her skin," he said, "she could just as easily have bled other places—her head, kidneys, spleen, liver. We'll have to wait and see."

I stared at the tube sewn into her neck. It was hard to believe that only two hours before—that two hours could make such a difference. God, I thought, even with doing everything it can still happen so quick.

The daytime staff had come on while the three of us were cleaning up, and now Mrs. Gowan joined us and helped Chris finish charting all the meds we'd given. McMillan asked her to get a nurse to special Mary the rest of the day.

"Have you called the parents?" she asked.

"Haven't had a chance," McMillan said. "I'll call them now, on my way to X ray."

It was past eight and I was already far behind schedule for drawing the morning bloods, but I stayed to help Chris clean Mary. Together we washed off the blood and alcohol stains, and while I looked for a clean pair of pajamas Chris combed out the dried blood from Mary's hair and braided it into little wings. I thanked her for all her help and wanted to say more but she was not in a mood to talk as she quietly went about doing what had to be done.

I left the room feeling completely drained, emotionally and physically. Even before the call about Mary had come in I had felt bone-tired. Now, with all that had happened and hardly any rest in the past twenty-four hours, I had the whole ward facing me again, including drawing the bloods.

And yet the realization that Mary was alive partly because of me, because of what we had done, gave me a kind of buoyancy. In the last analysis, it made all other concerns meaningless. It kept me going; it kept all of us going. The thought that at any other time in history she'd have died, that so many of our patients—but for us and what we had been able to do for them—would be dead, gave us our pride. It gave us a belief in medicine, plus a kind of unquestioning certainty that what we were doing and how we were doing it was right and unchallengeable. It was what our professors trumpeted, what they'd sold to us as medicine, and, like the very breaths our patients drew, it became the only touchstone of success and failure.

20

Mrs. Gowan couldn't get a special until noon; in the meantime she put an aide in to watch Mary. Neither McMillan nor I was satisfied with this arrangement, so we took turns checking Mary ourselves. I had just looked at her and was about to leave her room when the Berquams walked in. Damn it, I thought, a few seconds more and I'd've been in the clear. I mumbled hello and went on putting my things back into my case.

Mrs. Berquam, too troubled to speak, remained standing in the doorway. Her husband stood opposite me by the bed, his eyes fixed on the blotches of discolored skin on his child's face and arms. Shaking his head, he stared at the IV bottle and the drops dripping slowly into the tubing, then looked closely at where we had cut into her neck.

"Idiot," he said, so softly he might have been talking to himself, and raising his eyes to me, in a voice that was ominously calm, he added: "You stupid, blundering idiot."

"Herb!" Mrs. Berquam said, starting toward him in alarm.

Her husband ignored her. "You stupid goddamn fool," he said. "Have you done enough now?" And raising his voice menacingly: "Well, have you?"

"Please, Herb, stop," Mrs. Berquam pleaded.

"Me stop!" he burst out. "Me! Is this what you wanted?" He seized her hand and dragged her over to the bed. "Look at your child. See what they've done to her." He pulled back the sheet. "Go on, look at her."

"My God!" Mrs. Berquam moaned. "Oh, my God!"

I grabbed the sheet from his hand. "What the hell—"

"Shut up!" he hissed through clenched teeth.

His wife was sobbing now, with her fists pressed tightly against her mouth.

"Berquam," I said, "I want you out of here. Just get the hell out of here. Now!"

"Why, you arrogant young—"

I guess I saw it coming, but either I didn't believe it possible or was too hemmed in between Berquam and the bed to move. I got my arm up but his fist skidded off my forearm and caught me on the side of the jaw, snapping my head around. The second blow landed on my shoulder. In the confusion of the moment I saw McMillan hurrying into the room, with others crowding behind him.

"Hold it!" McMillan said.

Berquam turned from me. "You sonofabitch!" he cried,

"are you satisfied now? Look at her. Look!" His voice bounced off the walls and out into the corridor. "Haven't you tortured her enough?"

Without warning he hurled himself on McMillan and the two men hit the floor. I heard a sharp crack. Berquam was on top and getting ready to swing when I seized his arm. At the same time somebody grabbed me from behind. Twisting around I caught whoever it was with my elbow. McMillan managed to push Berquam off him, but before he could get up Berquam was on him again, punching him in the face. I swung at Berquam and got hit myself. Stunned, out of the corner of my eye I saw Handelman, with blood gushing from his nose, getting ready to swing again. But suddenly there were arms around him and others were grabbing Berquam and me.

"Let me go," Berquam screamed hysterically, struggling to free himself. "Look what they've done to her. She's dead. Can't they see it? She's dead. She's dead. Don't they know it? She's dead. She's dead. She's dead."

Mrs. Gowan was the one who straightened things out and got the ward functioning again. Within minutes she had the hallway cleared, parents and visitors back into their own rooms, and the ward looking as if nothing unusual had happened. She had Mrs. Berquam taken to an empty room and gave her a sedative herself, had an aide take Handelman down to radiology to have his nose x-rayed, and called one of the psychiatric residents down to see Berquam. McMillan had to have the inside of his mouth stitched up. As for me, except for a feeling of confusion and a couple of bruises, I was okay if still stunned.

Prader of course found out what had happened, and within a half hour was on the ward. He talked with Mrs. Gowan and apparently tried to talk to Berquam who refused to see him. I expected to find Prader angry, even furious, but he was quite calm even when he talked to us. It was plain, though that he was put out, that the edge was on.

"I know how it ended," he said dryly. "How did it begin?"

McMillan told him about Mary's vomiting and aspirating, the respiratory arrest, the intravascular consumption and its treatment. He reported on the lab values, the medications and their dosages, the route of administration, the cut-down, the central venous pressure, the arrhythmias, and transfusions.

Prader seemed to be studying me while McMillan was talking, but I felt too exhausted to react or care. To hell with it, I thought. We'd done what had to be done, and we'd done it right. What happened wasn't our fault.

"The real problem," McMillan said, "was that the Berquams got into the room before I could talk with them. I called them, but they had already left for the hospital. I didn't see them when they came in. They went directly to their daughter's room. I didn't have a chance to warn them, or even tell them what had happened."

"Why didn't you call them last night?" Prader said, "or early this morning when you realized she was becoming worse?"

"We were working. I called them the first chance I got."

"Then why didn't you have the nurse call, or an orderly?"

Jesus Christ, I thought, what's this, the third degree or something? McMillan just looked at Prader a moment, and then said calmly: "I was busy. All my thoughts and energy were centered on saving her life."

I thought Prader was going to go after him. Instead he turned to me, and I told him what had happened in the room.

"I was standing there, about to leave," I explained, "when Berquam came at me. He just freaked out. I guess I blocked the first punch, but he kept coming. The second one glanced off the side of my head. Then Dr. McMillan came in and he turned on him."

"And Mrs. Berquam?"

"She tried to stop her husband, but he just pulled the sheets off the patient and asked his wife if that's what she wanted. It would have made any mother hysterical."

"And what did you do then?" Prader asked.

"What do you mean?" I asked.

Prader ignored my belligerent tone. "I asked what you did then."

"I took the sheet away from him."

"And Mr. Handelman?"

"I was trying to help McMillan. I swung around and I guess I hit Handelman with my elbow."

"Breaking his nose is hardly helping Dr. McMillan."

"He was trying to get Berquam off me," McMillan said.

"He can speak for himself," Prader snapped.

I resented the inquisition. "Hitting Handelman was an accident," I said angrily. "My only concern was to get McMillan free of Berquam and I'd do it again if I had to."

Prader looked at McMillan. "Do you agree with that? Hitting him if it happened again?"

The question was so unexpected it caught us both off-guard.

"Well, doctor, I'm waiting," Prader said. "Never mind— From now on I want to know about any change in the patient's condition. And I want you to check with me about any change in her orders. Any change. Is that understood."

Afterwards I thanked McMillan for trying to bail me out.

"It's OK," he said, calmly as if nothing had happened.

The ward didn't settle down. It's not every day that you have a brawl in a patient's room, not every day that doctors are attacked and parents injured. The tension remained. And it was growing; I could see it in the looks we got. I found myself having to explain things two or three times and even then, in some cases, I could only get a provisional kind of acceptance. Several parents demanded to see a staff man before they would sign an operative permit or agree to a procedure no matter how small. Even the most cooperative parents seemed suddenly to view all of us with caution. The whole situation made me uncomfortable, as I knew it did Lang.

McMillan acknowledged there was a problem but shrugged it off. "Any time a system breaks down, or shows signs of strain—especially one as important and intricate as medicine—there's bound to be a period of confusion," he explained. "It makes people leery. But it will pass. Don't let it bother you."

But it did bother us. For Lang and myself it was becoming a trial just to walk on the ward. Mrs. Gowan, too, was feeling the pressure, spending a great deal of time just trying to keep the peace between the parents and us. Some of the nurses, especially the older ones like Barbara, were as concerned as we were and sympathized with us, while others like Chris said nothing.

Chris was in the room with me when a mother asked for a weekend pass for her child. "You're not doing anything but taking her temperature and giving her pills," the mother said. "I can do that myself."

I explained why her daughter had to stay, that we had to watch her blood pressure. "It may not seem as if we're doing much, but we are," I said and I went over the whole thing again; what we were doing and why, the need for taking temps and blood pressures. Finally I managed to convince the mother that her child should stay. And all the time Chris went on with what she was doing, offering no help or support.

"I could have used you on my side," I said when we left the room.

"I'm not on any side," she said. "I just listen."

"So you think that's enough, just to listen." She was about to turn away when I grabbed her arm. "For Chrissake," I said, "it's like pulling teeth. This place is becoming a real burden. What's going on is interfering with everything. If you like listening, then listen. I could grind out the next couple of weeks here making like I was blind and deaf, but I don't want to play games."

Chris looked at me searchingly.

"We had a good ward," I said. "What's happening?"

"Can't you see for yourself?"

"I can see Berquam's stirring them up."

"Oh, for God's sake! They're not children. Do you think Braden gave Mrs. Gowan an argument because Mr. Berquam talked him into it? That the Handelmans are bitter because Mr. Berquam told them things they didn't know?"

"Well, he sure doesn't help any," I said.

"He's not the problem. Take Mr. Berquam off this ward and the parents would still feel the same way. Yes, they would and they'd still be abused in the same way. They'd still be intimidated in the same way. They'd still be angry."

"What are you talking about?" I said with some heat.

"You said you wanted to know what was happening, didn't you? Do you think Mr. Braden blew up over a stupid ten or fifteen minutes of visiting rights? Or that Mr. Handelman's worried about Freddy not getting the care he needs? Nonsense. He's worried, alright, but not about whether the catheter's in the right place or the ALG's the right dose. What's eating him is how in heaven's name he's going to get the money to keep paying for his child's care. How's he going to pay for another transplant with what his insurance covers. Have you, or Lang, or McMillan, ever asked him how he feels about going through the whole thing all over again?"

I was about to protest, but Chris had the bit in her teeth and nothing could stop her.

"It's like the Berquams," she said. "For some reason you all seem to feel that everything begins and ends here on the ward. You're wrong. These parents go home. They have other lives, other feelings, other concerns. Take one instance: Did any one of you know that Mrs. Berquam is pregnant?"

"That's not our concern," I said.

"Obviously not."

"Damn it, we do talk to them. You know we do."

"Well, you don't do it very well. Some of these kids—especially the older ones—feel so guilty about their illness, the burden they are to their families. Holidays their brothers can't take because all the money goes to pay hospital bills. The new car the family can't buy because they have to pay for a new heart valve. These kids see how worried their fathers are about bills, and they get so depressed, some of them, they wish they were dead. They don't take their medications, they don't follow advice, they don't stick to their diets.

"Not a day goes by when the nurses and even the aides aren't asked questions that you doctors should have answered. Or at the very least been aware of. If you don't think those concerns affect patient care, you're crazy."

"It's not that we aren't always available," I said. "I've never ignored a question, nor has McMillan, or Lang, or anyone I know of."

"Sure. You talk to them about sodiums, potassiums, urine culture results, and all the rest, and they don't understand what you're talking about. You don't answer a damn thing, actually. You're all so smug and self-centered and unapproachable that most parents are just plain afraid to ask you about the things that really bother them. The little things that mean so much. They're afraid you'll laugh at them."

"For God's sake, Chris," I protested, "we're not mind readers."

"Oh, come off it," she said. "You don't have to be a mind reader to know how much depression, how much anxiety, anger, and guilt there is out there. The only thing that's preventing a real revolt is that eventually most get a little of what they want. Their kids get better soon enough. As for the rest, it's only fear that keeps them in line. If you get angry with them, they've got no place to go."

We had over twelve hundred admissions a year and most parents left realizing that we'd done all we could and their children had got the best medical care available. There would always be those who left unhappy or disgruntled or angry. I felt that Chris had gone off the deep end. Still, if she felt so strongly that we weren't handling things right I was willing to give it a try. I was all for doing anything to make it easier for the parents—and for me.

It was like falling into a bureaucratic nightmare. Little things I thought could easily be done became impossible to accomplish. When parents complained about having to wait so long to see the surgeons I tried to help by paging them myself. I might have spared myself the effort. I only succeeded in angering two of the chief residents who told me to quit paging them, they would come when they were ready. And when I tried to facilitate work-ups, the X-ray department refused to schedule two procedures the same day or do anything on Saturdays.

The nursing office was opposed to allowing patients on medications to leave for overnight stays, and the administration absolutely refused to sanction passes for more than twenty-four hours. "If you want to let them go for over twenty-four hours," I was told, "you will have to discharge them and readmit them."

Laboratories closed at three in the afternoon, which made it necessary to keep the patient another day at $140 for a follow-up lab test, rather than discharge him and have him brought back the next day. With most fathers working and families having only one car, there was no way the patient could be brought back to the hospital before three, so we had to keep him.

I began to see that in a very real sense the hospital was run for the people who worked in it, rather than for the patients. I had never thought of this before, and even now it was hard to accept, but there it was.

21

Like a fairy princess, Mary stayed in her trance, unwaking and unwakeable. Her skin lesions began to fade, but aside from that she did not respond. Watching her, it was as if her frail stricken body was struggling desperately and alone to put itself in order.

There were times when it seemed she was close to waking. "Mary," I would whisper as I stood by her bed, "Mary," imploring her in my heart to wake. At times I felt she heard me; her eyelids fluttered, but her eyes remained closed. She seemed so close to waking in those tense quiet moments.

We did two more spinal taps. McMillan called Prader about the first one. Judging by how long he stayed on the phone, I thought there must have been some kind of argument.

"Something wrong?" I asked when he hung up.

"No—not really."

"What do you mean, not really? I don't like this being in the middle without knowing what's going on. Prader's not the easiest guy to read but it's obvious he's not pleased. You were on the phone quite a while. Doesn't he want us to do the spinal tap?"

"He agreed," McMillan said.

"Agreed! That means—"

"Like you said, he's impossible to read."

"I said difficult, not impossible."

"Come on," McMillan said. "Let's get the tap done."

He let me do the tap while he held Mary steady. Every tube filled with blood. Unhappily, I held them up one at a time to show him; the last one was as bloody as the first.

"She bled into her skin, why not into her brain?" he said, "same process, only different organs."

At the time I resented his callousness, though when I think of it now I doubt it was that; I think he was just better at hiding his feelings than I was.

There were no white cells in the spinal fluid, and the smear was negative for bacteria. We kept on with the IV antibiotics and talked about taking out the central venous pressure.

"I don't know," McMillan said. "We should get it out soon. It's a source of infection. But then—"

"Sometimes she looks pretty good," I ventured.

"Better keep it in," he said.

At first I refused to accept the implication of the spinal tap. I told myself we didn't actually know how bad the bleed was, what areas of the brain had been irreversibly injured and which ones might come back after the bleeding and swelling subsided. There had been cases of recovery after intracranial hemorrhages. We'd have to wait and see.

That afternoon we got an EEG and it showed a diffuse, markedly abnormal pattern, but I still kept up my hope. Even unconscious Mary was definitely looking better. Little by little the color was coming back to her cheeks. It takes time, I thought.

Two days later, we did a second tap. I didn't ask McMillan if he had talked with Prader. I assumed he had.

The spinal fluid was a little clearer, but not much. Reluctantly I had to face the fact that Mary's skin was not her brain, that unlike a skin cell once a brain cell was dead it was dead forever. Yet I continued to grasp at any straw of improvement. And there were some. Her vital signs stabilized, the cardiac monitor began to show normal patterns, and her respirations, though weak, were adequate.

But when we took the catheter out of her bladder she didn't void, and throughout the rest of the day her bladder, like a balloon, began growing till it filled the whole lower part of her abdomen. We had to catheterize her again. There was no response from her even to the pain of the catheter being put back. She lay there unmoving, while I poked and pulled.

A short while afterwards Mrs. Berquam came on the ward. When she caught sight of me she tried to smile, but her smile quickly faded, and as she approached I could see how exhausted she looked, how drained. Her makeup, always so precise and understated, that day seemed a kind of afterthought that only accentuated the dark hollows under her eyes.

She knew about the taps, which surprised me since McMillan had not telephoned. "Better to leave things alone and not call," he said. At the time I thought Chris must have called her, or Mrs. Gowan; later I learned it was Prader.

"Mary's the same," I said, and added to sound encouraging, "her spinal fluid is clearing though." I was about to explain what the clearing could mean when she stopped me.

"Can I see her?" she asked.

I said, "Of course," but she hesitated a moment and I felt she was fearful.

"Mary really looks better," I said. "Honest. She's still unconscious, but at times she's almost awake."

Mrs. Berquam sat by her child's bed most of the afternoon. Several times I looked in on her but she sat there as unmoving as the patient. Once I thought I heard her talking softly to Mary but I couldn't be sure. The room was darkening when I finally joined her to talk about her daughter. I was about to turn on the light when I thought better of it and went over to the foot of the bed.

For a while there was silence between us and then I heard Mrs. Berquam remark quietly, "This isn't a real life, is it?" Suddenly I understood it was not hope she wanted, that at times hope was not enough. Such a thought had never occurred to me before, but it has remained with me ever since.

"No, it is not a real life," I said.

"Yet she can live like this."

"Yes. We can keep feeding her IV and giving her medications."

Mrs. Berquam looked at her daughter sadly. "She doesn't even know I'm here."

"No," I said, knowing I was shutting another door on her.

"Then maybe—I mean, why shouldn't I go home? I have other things to do," she added guiltily. "My husband. I have other children—"

"I think you should go home," I said.

Mrs. Berquam rose slowly from her chair, cramped by hours of sitting in the same position, and as I watched her get stiffly to her feet I thought, sooner or later, for every dying child, somebody has to take the responsibility of telling the parents the only thing left for them to do is to go home.

22

Another day, and Lang blew his stack. "That sonofabitch!" he swore, talking about a Mr. Bera, the father of one of his patients. "He wants to know if I'm sure penicillin will work. If we shouldn't try something more powerful. If *I'm* sure! A fucken cab driver asking *me* about penicillin."

He was so angry he even said it in front of two aides. Not that everybody working in the hospital didn't already know what was happening on 402. It was the gossip of every ward. The other house staffs were cautious about openly discussing the situation with us; some even seemed to go out of their way to avoid mentioning it. But apparently they began to act differently on their own wards. We heard that the other interns and residents were making an effort to change things, taking longer with their interviews, explaining in some cases at great length the problems of the hospital system even if they personally didn't consider them to be deficiencies at all, reminding the parents of new patients that they were always available if anything went wrong. They might have agreed with us and been sympathetic, but they acted as if what was happening on 402 was contagious and might spread.

The next day Lang exploded. He had been on call the whole night taking care of a new diabetic in coma. In the morning he'd taken a shower to wake up but when he got to rounds it was plain he was all in. Still, he'd managed to draw all his bloods before going downstairs to get some coffee. It was when he came back and was reexamining the Bera child and the father began again questioning him about adding another drug to the treatment that he blew up. According to Mrs. Gowan he told Bera that if he didn't like the care his son was getting or felt it wasn't the best available he could goddamn well just leave and take his kid somewhere else.

I was down in the lab at the time checking some urine cultures. When I came back I found the normally even-tempered Mrs. Gowan fuming.

"What's wrong?" I said.

She had picked up the phone but now she slammed it down again. I had never seen her so angry.

"I really should," she said.

"Should what?"

"Some of you—" she said bitingly. "Honestly, sometimes I wonder who you think you are—Don't look so innocent. You know what I'm talking about. Now Mr. Bera wants to sign a complaint against Lang. I should let him do it, too. I still have a mind to call Dr. Prader and get Lang kicked off the ward." She told me what had happened.

"Cool it," I said. "Maybe Lang shouldn't have said what he did. But he's been up all night—"

"Don't give me that stuff. You don't fly off the handle just because you're tired."

"You sure that's all there is?" I said. "It's just Bera?—"

"What do you mean?" she asked, suddenly nervous, it seemed to me, which was as unusual for Mrs. Gowan as losing her temper was. "You just take care of your friend. I'll take care of Mr. Bera."

Nothing came of the whole thing, but it did raise the tension on the ward a degree higher. It was the surgeons, though, who provided the proverbial straw, changing the last bit of provisional acceptance that some of the parents still felt into overt distrust.

We had admitted a child with ulcerative colitis, a miserable, wasted kid with chronic bloody diarrhea, who hadn't responded to steroid therapy or enemas. At a combined surgical and pediatric conference the decision was made to remove his colon and do an ileostomy. Naturally, the parents weren't happy about it. The Thompsons were overprotective to begin with, and they hated the idea of their child for the rest of his life having to collect his stool in a bag clipped to his side. Eventually we prevailed after explaining at length that without the colectomy he would continue to bleed, to be malnourished, to have fevers, to be weak and irritable, and in the end the ulcerative colon itself, if not removed, would become cancerous and have to be removed anyway.

So the operation was scheduled, the permits were signed, and the patient was being readied for surgery the next morning, when the parents had second thoughts. They called me into their son's room, said they'd been talking to other parents and now they had some doubts about the necessity of surgery. I tried to convince them it had to be done; I went over the whole bit all over again, I assured them that after the operation they would have a happier child, but they insisted on seeing the surgeon.

I called Barmeister, the chief resident on the pediatric surgery service; he was the one who had initially talked to them about the operation and would be doing the surgery. He was in the OR and I left a message for him to call me. While we waited, the parents were getting more and more agitated. I kept telling them that Barmeister was busy but I could feel a head of steam building up and I called the paging operator again to tell Barmeister it was important. He called back a little after seven.

"They're having second thoughts," I said.

"The permits are signed," he said. "He's on schedule," as if that ended any further discussion.

"But they still want to talk to you."

"Can't you talk to them?" he said, testily.

"They want you."

"Damn it, I'm busy."

"So am I. They want to see you. You're doing the surgery, remember? Not me."

"Can't you control the patients on your own ward?" He sounded as disgusted as I was annoyed.

"When can I tell them you'll be here?" I said, ignoring his comment. "It's almost the end of visiting hours."

"When I'm free," he said, slamming down the phone.

I was pretty sore, but I tried not to show it. I told the parents that Barmeister had an emergency admission and would be further delayed, but they could stay after hours until he came.

An hour later I saw Wagner, a second year resident on pediatric surgery, come on the ward, and I went to stop him before he reached the Thompsons.

"Look, Bill," I said, "it would take too long to explain, but they don't want you."

"Barmeister told me to talk to them."

"I know, but we've been having a bit of a problem up here, and you're not going to be of help."

Wagner shrugged. "Barmeister's not going to like this," he said.

Barmeister came up a few minutes later. He didn't even look at me, just walked right past me into the Thompsons' room. I guess he tried to bowl them over, but it didn't work. After staying in the room for quite some time he left looking disgusted, with the Thompsons following him out. From where I was sitting in the doctors' station I could see Handelman approaching from the other end of the corridor.

Barmeister stopped by the station. "It's up to you," he said brusquely. "I've told you what you could expect. If you want to accept the responsibility that's OK with me. But he'll still have to be operated on sooner or later, and now is the best time. He's as healthy as he'll ever be."

"That's not the point, is it?" I heard Handelman say. He had joined the Thompsons and was standing close by, listening.

Barmeister swung around, surprised. "Who are you?" he said.

"A friend," Handelman said.

"Well, this is between these parents and myself."

"A little one-sided, isn't it?"

"We want him here," Thompson said.

Evidently nothing like this had ever happened to Barmeister before. He looked simply amazed as Handelman questioned him now.

"What are the chances of their son's colon becoming cancerous. And at what age? When you take out that colon it's forever, you know. Isn't there any new research being done now that might be applicable in the next five or ten years? I mean research that would cure their son and still allow him to keep his colon and not have to use a bag to collect his feces for the next forty years of his life?"

Barmeister must have felt himself cornered. He looked from one to the other, intermittently startled, uncomfortable and angry.

I knew what he was feeling: what the hell's going on here? Parents questioning him? Asserting themselves? Giving him advice? It was simply unheard of.

All throughout training—surgeons and physicians alike—patients had been paraded before us as specimens. "And now a diabetic—Be sure to check her eyes to see the retinal degeneration—You'll soon be seeing an interesting case of sickle cell anemia—There are four types of hydrocephalus in infants; the one that will be presented today is of the obstructive type—"

At conferences patients would sit nervous and humble, waiting for their turn. In clinics they were presented half naked, in closed little rooms where instructors pointed out this or that without a thought of ever mentioning what the patient might be feeling about his illness, or even his name. The patients were not there to ask questions or, in fact, to speak at all. No wonder any sign of a patient or parent asserting himself was viewed by us at best with suspicion, and at worst with outright anger.

In any event, Barmeister left without bothering to answer Handelman. The child was not operated on; Barmeister called the staff man and they decided to cancel the procedure.

I'd like to think it was not a matter of pique, or punishment. Whatever it was, Barmeister and the staff surgeon hid behind the argument that you don't operate and make yourself legally responsible without authorization and complete agreement of the patient or the patient's representative. But at the time I was angry. As I told McMillan: "The Thompsons were close to agreeing. All they wanted was a little reassurance. There was no reason for Barmeister blowing it the way he did. None."

"Don't worry," McMillan said.

"But things are getting worse."

"No matter. It will end."

"You sound so sure."

"I'm not pleased with it, but it'll burn itself out. We do a good job. In the end, that's what counts."

"And meanwhile, in the short term?" I said. "I mean like the next two weeks. Till I get off this damn ward."

"Patients come and go," McMillan said. "There's no real constituency. There never is among the ill, and never will be."

The canceling of the operation and the flap it caused among the surgeons brought us a visit from most of the full-time pediatric staff. The professors in the department, like everybody else in the hospital, must have known what was happening on 402, but it took the cancellation of Thompson's surgery with the disruption in the OR schedule, and the complaints about it from the surgical staff, to bring them onto the ward.

"Showing the flag," Lang called it. "You think they'd remind the parents they were only hurting themselves," he said. "It's their own kids who will suffer. Start changing everything for everybody and it's going to be a mess. Nobody will know what the hell is happening or what to expect. They're interfering with their own kids' best interests."

Showing the flag was all it was. I could see now that McMillan had some justification for his complaint about the professors. They were faced with a situation they couldn't handle—a bit more of the whole man than they were used to.

With the same display of concerned disinterest that allowed other members of the house staff to grumble about the parents on our ward while they changed their attitude toward the parents on theirs, the professors walked around in their starched white coats, looked at a few charts, talked with some of the parents and joked with others—and blamed us.

A few settled for just strutting and disappearing, as if their appearance by itself would set everything right; others were obviously annoyed that they had to come down at all. Most let us know they felt the problem on 402 was our fault, that we had handled everything wrong, and that if we hadn't everything would be as right as it had always been. I was surprised at how vehement some of them were about this.

McMillan stood his ground. "The parents aren't altogether wrong," he said. "Give us better staffing, more nurses, more doctors; cut down the waiting; let's have better lab services, and surgeons who come by when they say they will, and more time to spend with patients. Then maybe things will get better."

Unlike the other professors, Prader tried to do something about the situation; at least he didn't merely come by and then disappear. He asked McMillan to name those parents who were causing the most trouble. He was as cold as I had ever seen him; I thought any other resident might well have crumbled under that gaze, but McMillan calmly listed those parents he felt were most involved.

I dismissed Prader's concern as simply his usual direct way of attacking a problem—any problem.

There was no mistaking the look on his face, though, when he came out of Mary's room. He was angry. At the same time he was surprisingly defensive, almost cautious with me.

"Where's Dr. McMillan?" he asked.

"He's gone down to a conference," I said.

"Has she responded at all?"

"No, sir. But her vital signs are stable."

"What about her EEG?"

"It's diffusely abnormal."

"And the neurologist's interpretation?"

I hesitated. "Diffuse brain damage—But—"

"And your plans?"

"Mine?"

"Yes, yours. You're taking care of her, aren't you? You and Dr. McMillan."

"Yes, sir."

"Then you do have a plan? Or are you just going to handle things as they come along?"

"Support her," I said.

"And for how long?" Prader said, staring me down.

"I'm afraid I don't understand."

"How long are you going to keep supporting her? A week? A month?"

"As long as we have to, I suppose."

Apparently he had heard enough, for he made no further comment, but turned on his heel and walked away.

"Did Prader talk to you?" I asked McMillan later.

"Yeah."

"What's going on?" I asked. "He's pretty disturbed."

"Pressures," McMillan said. "Prader's a great man, and he's got a difficult job. Did he argue about Mary? How long to treat her?"

"In a way. He's not one to argue much."

"He runs a big department," McMillan said thoughtfully. "How many leukemics does he take care of? A hundred, a hundred and twenty-five? Plus his research program? Plus his teaching? Even for somebody like him it's hard to keep driving all the time."

"So you think the protocol he sent down—"

"It was appropriate."

"Sure," I said, "but you wanted more."

"No—It would probably be more accurate to say I couldn't find a reason why more shouldn't be done."

"So you decided?—I mean, did you actually think Prader was shortchanging the patient? Giving her less than adequate therapy?"

"It doesn't matter what I thought. The protocol might have been better. That's arguable. We had no control over that. The important thing is since then we've been doing everything that we should be doing. That's what counts—You look surprised."

I hesitated. "I guess I am," I said finally.

McMillan shrugged. "The father didn't want her treated. She was desperately ill. And remember, she wasn't on the study. Everyone could do what he wanted. No more rules."

"So when she started to go sour you decided to make sure that nobody would shortchange her again, or could. Not Prader, not her parents. Nobody."

"Preventive medicine," McMillan said. "Right or wrong, you don't lose either way."

But what if he was right? It was hard to believe that Prader would ever do less than the maximum, that any doctor would, for that matter, much less Prader. He wasn't the type to be rattled or pushed into doing what he didn't want to do or what he felt was wrong.

Yet even as I thought about it, Prader's question: "How long are you going to support her?" kept surfacing in my mind.

23

If Mary had died right then and there—or begun to improve even the slightest—things would have settled down, not only for the ward but for me too. I would have been able to dismiss my own concerns and confusion by simply going on.

But Mary didn't die. She just lay there and, in a sense, kept the whole thing going. True, the problems of the ward had taken on a momentum of their own, but her presence fed it. Parents of the new patients stopped talking when they passed her room; those who had been on the ward for some time pointedly ignored it. And I was plagued seeing her unmoving day after day, watching her mother barely able to bring herself to walk into the room, knowing her father was hiding somewhere.

Had we performed a miracle, or taken part in a disaster?

The extraordinary thing was that despite all that was happening—or not happening—I was still expecting some kind of improvement in Mary—in fact counting on it. Didn't we have all of science and medicine working for us?

In addition to examining Mary twice a day, morning and evening, I looked in on her before going to my room when I was on call to make sure the IV was fixed properly into her vein and running well. There weren't many veins left to use and we didn't want to lose any more than we had to.

It was about ten o'clock when Barbara called me to tell me there was something wrong with Mary.

"Her heart has speeded up a little," she said when I joined her in the nurses' section. "Just a little," she added, seeing the anxiety in my face, "but it's a pretty constant elevation."

"How fast?"

"It's been seventy, seventy-five. It's eighty-five now."

"Her fluids."

"Right on schedule."

Outwardly Mary's condition seemed unchanged, but her pulse was eighty-five and the change in her respirations worried me. The change was subtle but I had watched her so intently for so long I knew they weren't the same.

"Thanks, Barbara, I'll check her over," I said, and waited for her to leave the room. I wanted to be alone with Mary. I lifted her arm out from under the sheet. It was warmer than I expected. Even with her lying perfectly still her pressure was elevated. Ill at ease I checked the vital-signs chart on the wall; all her preceding blood pressures were normal. I stared at the straight lines, the days of straight lines—the heart rates, blood pressures, and respirations—which ran unerringly hour after hour across the chart.

And in the silence of the moment I knew, as surely as I had ever known anything, that Mary would never wake again.

"What was her last blood pressure?" I asked Barbara when I came back to the nurses' station.

"Hundred ten, hundred twenty, over eighty," she said.

"Well, it's up now. Who's the neurology resident on call?"

"Dr. Brown, I think. I'll find out. What do you think's wrong?"

"Her head. Increased intracranial pressure. Pressing on her brain stem affecting the nerve centers that control her respiration and blood pressure. Her lungs are clear. The last chest film was negative. There's no other reason except her brain for her breathing to change or her blood pressure to fluctuate."

In a few minutes Brown came in. I gave him Mary's history and said what I thought was wrong. After examining her he agreed there probably was increased pressure.

"Since she's bled into her head," he said, "the clots could be breaking up and swelling, causing the pressure to increase."

"What would you do?" I asked.

He shrugged. "Watch her. If she gets worse—glycerol, maybe mannitol. I'd cut back on the IV fluids and run her a bit dry."

"How will we know?" I said. "I mean about her getting worse."

Brown looked at me strangely. "More fluctuation in her blood pressure and respiration. Her heart may become erratic—speeding up, slowing down. Her pupils will dilate—she has to be watched, and closely. It can go quick; the brain stem can herniate in minutes—Those fading blotches on her body?"

"Purpura. She bled into her skin."

"She has leukemia—right?" Brown gave me that look again. I knew what he was thinking. "OK," he said finally. "I'll be on all night. If anything changes give me a call."

As he was leaving, Barbara walked in, obviously disturbed.

"Excuse me," she said, "but Mr. Bera doesn't want to leave."

"What's that?" I said.

"Visiting hours are over and he won't leave."

"Barbara," I said wearily, "we're going to need a special nurse for Mary."

"But visiting hours are over," she insisted.

"For Chrissake," I said. "I don't give a good goddamn if he stays all night."

"But—"

"But nothing. If you're so concerned, call Mrs. Gowan. I don't want to hear anything more about it. We need a special now. Can we get one?"

The nursing office reported it was too late to get one before the night shift; those nurses who had been available had already been assigned to other wards.

"I'll watch her myself," I said to Barbara.

The ward was quiet, and after calling the ER to make sure there were no admissions coming up I took a couple of the journals I was going to read anyway and went back to Mary's room.

Leaving the main light off I adjusted the small wall lamp so I could read by it, and sat down by the bed, opening to an article I had to read. But my eyes were on Mary. If you didn't know she had not moved, or uttered a sound, or opened her eyes in over a week, you'd have said she was sleeping peacefully.

Through the partly open door muted night sounds filtered into the room. Nights on a ward, even a busy ward, are always quiet periods. There is a kind of hush that hovers over everything; it is as if you can almost hear the ward breathing. Kids who during the day cry out for attention, seem only to whimper at night. Concerns that appear so glaring and critical in the light lose their edge in the dark, become needs rather than urgencies. Everyone seems so alone, so separate.

I tried to read, but it was no go, and I sat there with the journal open in my lap watching Mary lying in the shadow beyond the light of the wall lamp. She really did look like a sleeping princess. Only I was no prince, there were no magic potions any more, and no kiss could wake her. I watched her breathing until I seemed to be breathing for her.

The voice of the paging operator cut through the silence. What was I doing sitting here? I wondered; what did I hope to accomplish? I was simply there, as people had always been there with the dying, so those they cared about, those they loved, would not be alone.

I was holding Mary's hand when the door opened wider. I thought it was Barbara coming to tell me about a new admission or an IV that had infiltrated, but it was Mrs. Gowan.

"So you're the new special nurse," she said softly, as she came into the room.

Embarrassed I let go of Mary's hand. "Yeah," I said self-consciously, "I guess I am."

Mrs. Gowan went over to the foot of the bed and I looked at her as if I was seeing her for the first time. I had never seen her out of uniform before, had never thought of her as other than a nurse. She was wearing slacks and a fluffy pullover sweater, and her dark hair fell straight and loose to her shoulders. She was lovely.

"You came because of Bera?" I said. "I'm sorry."

"That's alright," she said. "He's on his way now." She moved to the side of the bed opposite where I was sitting. "How's she doing?"

"Worse," I said. "She's not going to make it."

I expected some kind of objection, some argument, but Mrs. Gowan made no comment.

"You knew it without my telling you, is that it?" I said when she still remained silent. "Why didn't you say something?"

She smoothed the sheet around Mary's shoulders. "What was there to say? You're not children. I can't tell you what to see."

She spoke without rancor, yet suddenly I felt betrayed. All the time we were congratulating ourselves on the miracle we had performed, she and Chris and God knows who else were shaking their heads behind our backs.

"That business of the parents. You were part of it, weren't you? I mean you knew all about what was going on, that Chris was supporting Berquam and the rest, yet you let it go. You could have helped."

"How?"

"You could at least have turned Chris off and withdrawn a kind of professional approval of their attitude. It would have made things easier for all of us."

I knew there was no point in my going after Mrs. Gowan like this, but I couldn't help myself. What was digging at me, I suppose, was the sense of my own helplessness, my recognition that we had failed.

"I have enough trouble," she said, "just keeping the ward going. Keeping it staffed and handling the more flagrant abuses of medical care. Like not enough nurses and aides. And doctors who forget that nurses can't be in two places at once. And schedules that are impossible for patients to keep. And night shifts that are unstaffable. Just keeping things together is a full-time job. The problem you're talking about isn't a nurse's problem."

"I know," I said. "I shouldn't have been accusing you. I'm sorry."

"Handelman will soon be gone. The others will have their kids discharged and things will be back to being pretty much the same as they've been before. It took somebody like Berquam who knows about hospitals and doctors to really push. And soon he'll be gone, too."

"Still you could have made it easier for all of us."

"I don't know if I wanted to," she said.

"But why? Why not?"

"Because," she said, "some day one of my children may be in a hospital."

24

We were on rounds the next morning when Chris came running out of Mary's room.

Mary had stopped breathing.

McMillan hurried into the room after Chris and we crowded after them. He was already breathing for Mary when Mrs. Gowan and Lang pushed in the emergency cart. I could see her chest rising and falling with each breath.

"She just stopped," Chris said. "Just like that. One minute she was breathing and the next she had stopped."

"How long?" I said.

"Ten seconds. Fifteen before I got to you."

Mrs. Gowan had half the emergency vials already opened. She handed me a syringe. "Bicarbonate," she said. "Ten cc's" and turned back to the cart to break open the rest of the meds.

Without waiting I picked up Mary's IV and emptied the syringe directly into her vein.

"Her heart's OK," Lang said, looking up from where he was kneeling by the bed, the stethoscope still in his ears.

McMillan kept breathing for Mary for another thirty seconds, then stopped.

"Hold it," Lang said. "Her heart rate's dropping."

"She's not breathing," I said. Her fingertips were turning blue.

Mrs. Gowan handed me another syringe of bicarbonate. I injected it while McMillan began breathing for Mary again and Lang continued to listen to her heart.

"It's back," he said.

But when McMillan stopped, the heart rate dropped again. He tried a third time and a fourth with the same results.

Lang shook his head. "It's no good," he said.

McMillan called for the endotracheal tube and Mrs. Gowan handed it to him along with the laryngoscope. Tilting back Mary's head he opened her mouth, and using the scope as a guide slipped the end of the tube down into her lungs and breathed quickly into it several times. Once again her chest moved with each breath.

"OK," Lang said, still listening.

"What's wrong?" Chris asked tensely.

"She won't breathe on her own," I said.

"What do you mean, won't?"

"Her brain. Something's happened to the cells in or near the area that controls breathing."

McMillan reached for the breathing bag, hooked the outlet over the tube, and began squeezing the bag. The valve popped in and out as he squeezed, hissing air into Mary's lungs.

"Give her some mannitol," he said to me. "Ten cc's per kilogram." And to Mrs. Gowan: "Call central supply for a respirator."

"Well," he said impatiently when Mrs. Gowan seemed to hesitate. "I can't squeeze this bag all day. Get a respirator."

"Will she ever be able to breathe again on her own?" Mrs. Gowan asked.

"Chris," McMillan ordered, "call central supply."

Confused, Chris looked from one to the other.

"You stay here," Mrs. Gowan said. "I'll call."

"Wait a minute," I said. "What are her chances? No, I mean it. What chance has she got?"

"None," McMillan said. "None, if we stop." He looked at Mrs. Gowan. "Go on," he said.

It took only a few minutes to hook the respirator up to the end of the endotracheal tube and adjust the flow rates and pressures so that the machine was working properly. I taped the tube down, crisscrossing Mary's jaw and nose with the tape. Lang and Chris removed the emergency cart and I finished up with McMillan who chose to ignore my silence. The only sound was the respirator hissing behind us.

"How much bicarbonate did you give her?" he asked finally.

I didn't have a chance to answer. McMillan was looking over my shoulder and when I turned around I saw Prader standing in the doorway. Mrs. Gowan was behind him. For a moment our eyes met, and then she was gone.

Prader looked at the two of us and then at the respirator. "Who ordered this?" he asked.

"I did," McMillan said.

"Why?"

"Why? Because it was called for."

Prader walked into the room. He glanced at Mary, then back at McMillan. "Don't you think it's time to stop being heroic?" he said.

"We've done nothing heroic," McMillan said. "She stopped breathing half an hour ago. Her heart rate stayed up as long as I breathed for her, so I put her on the respirator."

"Come now," Prader said. "Use your head. A child with leukemia, disseminated intravascular coagulation, meningitis, an intercerebral bleed, brain damage, unconscious for six days, irregular vital signs, a respiratory arrest, no spontaneous respirations after half an hour of resuscitation—"

"That's because of increased intracranial pressure," McMillan interrupted. "We've just given her mannitol. It will take a while."

"Don't you think enough is ever enough?"

"Enough?" McMillan echoed uncomprehending. For the first time since I had known him I saw him too surprised to speak. He stared at Prader's impassive face. "Enough!" he repeated after a moment's silence. "You of all people to talk about enough. I don't expect miracles, but I'm not going to stop using what's available. I'm not going to go back ten years for you or anybody."

Prader's face hardened. "And if she does wake up? And if you can get her off the respirator? What then?"

"Then she may have the same chance as any other child with leukemia."

"And if you're wrong? Would you wager five people's lives on being right?"

"I'm sorry," McMillan said. "I don't know what you mean."

"Are you blind?" Prader pointed to Mary. "What the hell do you think is happening to this child's family?"

"Her family! My God, look at your own clinic," McMillan said. "They're all dying and you keep giving them all those poisons week after week, trying to get another goddamn month out of them. Or is it a week? Or a day?"

Prader looked stunned. "You're not treating that child," he said icily, "you're treating yourself."

"Me! treating myself!" McMillan said bitterly. "I don't have any protocols to hide behind. I don't have any rigid rules to protect myself, scientific excuses of the greater good to get me off the damn hook. I'm here on the ward taking care of kids, not up in the lab tabulating figures."

It was as if Prader had been struck.

"And right now," McMillan kept after him, "I'm treating a very sick little girl. But she isn't dead. Not yet. I don't push a terminal case. But this girl isn't terminal. You can't tell me that tomorrow she won't be breathing again, or the next day. There's no reason not to use everything we have. That's why we're here. If we pull her through this she'll have a chance to lead some kind of life, not so different than a hell of a lot of kids in your own clinic. How many of them are going out of remission? How many are sick but still on protocols? How many are even past that, and still being given blood transfusions and antibiotics?"

For a moment there was silence, and the insistent mechanical hissing of the respirator took over the room.

When Prader spoke again he sounded strangely subdued. "It's not quite that simple," he said, almost as if he were talking to himself.

"When she's dead, she's dead," McMillan said. "That's simple enough. Then there is no chance, no hope, nothing. That's the real failure. I'm not going to kill her. If you want her dead you'll have to kill her yourself."

Prader stiffened. "We don't kill patients," he said.

"No? Then turn off the respirator."

While they were arguing, I saw blood beginning to ooze out of the corner of Mary's mouth. Fascinated, appalled, in the midst of all that was going on, all the paraphernalia, the tubes, the catheters, I watched the drop of blood gathering, growing, getting redder and redder, until like a tear it fell onto the endotracheal tube and began sliding slowly down the smooth gray-green plastic. And now another drop began to form, until like the first it left the corner of her mouth and began running down the tube.

I no longer heard what McMillan and Prader were saying. It was as if my own blood was oozing out of me, dropping onto that tube, and my chest felt heavy, as if the respirator was breathing for me. I wanted Mary to live, too, but not just for another day, another month, or even another year, not to have to crawl to watch other children playing as she had once been able to play herself, to have to struggle to think of a word, or just to keep milk in her mouth. I wanted her to be all that she could have been, all that was possible for her to be.

I watched the respirator driving her chest, mindlessly

pushing it in and out, and the sound of its hissing grew ever louder and louder, filling my head, filling all the room, drowning out what McMillan and Prader were saying. They stood facing each other across the bed, suddenly unreal, with expressions I couldn't read any more, words I couldn't understand.

I looked at Mary; her mouth taped, the tubes in her nose and mouth.

Enough, I thought. Enough. No more suffering. No more. No more.

I don't know if I said goodbye or thought it, nor to this day do I know if it was I who left Mary or she who left me. But I looked at her once again and for the last time, and I walked over to the wall and pulled the respirator plug.

The next thing I knew I was in the corridor walking towards the nurses' station. I saw Mrs. Gowan approaching me from the conference room. She stopped short.

"What's wrong?" she said. "You look so—"

"Nothing's wrong," I managed to say.

"Well—Mr. Berquam's here, and he's drunk and—"

"I'll see him."

"Maybe you shouldn't," she said. "He's pretty angry. It might be better if someone else talked to him."

"Talk, talk. That's part of the trouble, isn't it? Don't worry," I said. "Maybe this time I'll just listen."